Tales from
Aardvark County

As Told By
The Old-Timer

EDWIN GROVER LAWRENCE

Published by RSE Publishing
403 N. Harper Street, Laurens, SC 29360, U.S.A.

ISBN 978-0-9837103-4-9

Printed in the United States of America
Edited by Amanda L. Capps
Book Design by Michael Seymour

PUBLISHER'S NOTE

Dedication

I would like to dedicate this book to my wife Luanne, the love and inspiration of my life, who has worked hard to help me see this book to completion. Also I dedicate this book to the following people: Jan Williams – a friend, Bible scholar, and true servant of God. It was she who has given me words of encouragement concerning my writing for over thirty years. Jenny Stevens – a nurse and friend, whose life exemplified Christ daily as she worked. Bill Thomason – my pastor, who possesses an unusually large amount of wisdom in ministering to God's people. Alice Lawrence – my mother. Even though she had to quit school in the seventh grade to pick cotton, she saw a need for education, and she saw that all of her children went to school. (Actually, she sent me back to school on the second day even though I thought I was finished.)

Acknowledgements

I would like to take this opportunity to thank some of the nice folks who helped make this book possible:

A special thanks goes to my publicist, Amanda Capps, who convinced me that my writings were acceptable, and motivated me to actually get this book in print.

I would also like to thank everyone who ever told me a funny story or let me tell them one, especially all my classmates from the seventh grade on through college, who continually wrote in my yearbooks about my corny jokes.

I would like to thank my friend, Georgia Ricketts, who served as a technical advisor between my illustrator and me.

I would like to thank my friend, Sam Ricketts for the fine job he did illustrating my book.

I would like to thank my friend, Mike Workman, who taught me everything I know about bulls. (World's Oldest Profession story.)

Most of all, I would like to thank all the nice people at West End Baptist Church in Woodruff, SC, for their encouragement and support through the years. I thought I would have to wait until I got to heaven to see that many angels in one place, but I guess I was wrong.

Table of Contents

Introduction

When I was a junior in high school, it befell my lot in English class to do a book report. The book that I chose to read was John Steinbeck's *The Red Pony*. It was a story about a boy growing up on a horse ranch. In my report, I stated that I felt that the story had no plot. In my opinion, it was just a collection of short stories about events that happened in a young boy's life. My teacher did not like my report because she felt like I had bad-mouthed one of the great literary geniuses of all time. While I would not dare to compare myself to Mr. Steinbeck, I feel that his book and the one I have written have something in common. *Tales from Aardvark County* is also a collection of short stories, with no central theme or plot, about a fictional place called Aardvark County. The characters in this book are joined together only by the fact that they live in the same county. Many of them are further joined together by the fact that they attend the First Community Fellowship Church, where Rev. A.T. Laster is their beloved pastor.

According to the United States road atlas that I consulted, there is no such place as Aardvark County. It is merely a figment of the author's imagination. All other places mentioned in these stories are real. Also, the names of all churches and characters are also entirely fictional.

Believe me, I had a hard time thinking up all of these names. So, if when you read this book and find that a character's name is the same as yours, I sincerely apologize, but I also hope that you realize that it's your parents' fault as much as mine.

I have been telling jokes since I was in grade school. Probably seventy-five percent of the material in my book is original, made up out of my own brain matter. The other twenty-five percent is from jokes that I have heard along the way and put in my own words to make the book more enjoyable. I purposely have tried not to steal other people's stories and claim them as my own. I have the highest respect for other comedians' work. I was a big fan of the late Jerry Clower and am a fan of Jeff Foxworthy, but I did not include in my book, to my knowledge, any of their material, either spoken or written. It is best that redneck and coon-hunting stories be left to their original authors.

I have tried in this book to present situations that will make the reader laugh. I realize that some Christian people must think it is a sin to laugh or smile, but I don't see it that way. I don't believe Christian people should walk around with a sad face, looking like they could suck marbles out of a gopher hole. We need to lighten up! The truth of the matter is that funny things happen to everyone, even Christian people. Believe it or not, Christians, just like everyone else get in accidents, get gas, hemorrhoids, and even divorces. That's life. So I feel that if we are able to laugh at ourselves, and not take ourselves so seriously, then maybe we could be happier.

I make no apologies for the fact that my stories are

written from a Christian perspective. I could have written hundreds of stories if I had chosen to use a lot of vulgar language and cuss words, but I feel that we have enough of that already on the television and on the street. Besides, I don't talk that way, so I refuse to write that way.

These stories are what I like to call fictional reality. They are fiction, but they tell about realistic situations in life. There are no talking dogs, singing cats, or cows that can count to twenty. There are also no witches, goblins, vampires, or magical dragons. Those things are fantasy, not reality.

And so folks, may I present to you today *Tales from Aardvark County?* I sincerely believe that you will enjoy reading this book as much as I enjoyed writing it. In fact, I am willing to make you an unheard-of offer. If after you read this book, if it does not produce a chuckle or a smile, then I will gladly refund twenty-five cents of the purchase price (limit one offer per reader, please.) This offer is not valid if you bought this book at a yard sale or flea market, or if you received it as a gift.

May God bless! Keep smiling!

The Farmer and Mary-Juanita

Folks around here in Aardvark County call me the Old-timer. I guess that's because I have been living around here a long time. I've seen a lot of strange things happen, that looking back were quite comical. I would like to tell you about some of those happenings if you'd be so minded. What I want to tell you about first today is what happened down at the First Community Fellowship Church where Reverend A. T. Laster is the pastor. I mean no disrespect to the fine folks at the church, but I believe that sometimes if we could just learn to laugh at ourselves, then life could proceed a lot easier. Before I tell you what happened at the church though, I need to back up and tell you what brought all of this about.

It all started one summer a few years back, when I was resting on my front porch after working all day plowing with my mule in the field. I looked up and saw a strange looking person walking up the driveway. This man had on some ragged pants that looked like they might have been thrift store rejects. His hair was long, scraggly, and sweaty looking. He didn't have on a shirt as far as I could tell, but rather an old leather vest. His clothes were accessorized by a bag on his back and flip-flops on his feet. Looking back, I would have been a lot better off if I had just pretended

1

that I was deaf when he spoke, but I try not to be mean to people.

When this stranger came up and stood by the doorsteps, he said, "Hey there, Cool Daddy, could I trouble you for a glass of water?"

I looked straight at him and replied, "Son, I'll get you a glass of water, but it ain't cool; it is July, and I ain't your daddy."

When I returned with the water, he said "Thanks Cool Daddy."

Once again I reminded him, "It ain't cool; it's July and I sure ain't your daddy."

Then he began to talk about some crazy stuff. He asked me if I had ever smoked a roach. I told him, "I don't know what you do where you come from, but around here we don't smoke roaches. We step on them, or kill them with the aerosol spray."

Then he said, "No, Cool Daddy, you don't understand." After I had reminded him for the third time about the weather and his paternal ancestry, he explained to me what a roach was. Then he asked me, "Man how would you like to go in business with me? I have some seeds here that you can plant in your field, and in a few months when I come back, we can harvest a big cash crop."

Well, money had been kind of tight on the farm lately, so I took the seeds. I never did see that man again. I feel that he must have got in trouble with the law for arson, because before he left he mumbled something about burning a joint. For a while, I forgot what he had called those seeds, but I remembered they had a woman's name.

Then I remembered that he had called them Mary-Juanita. He hadn't told me who Mary or Juanita was, but I assumed that it must have been his mother and sister. I didn't see how anybody that looked like him could ever have a girlfriend or wife. I didn't know anything about growing Mary-Juanita, so I planted the seeds on the back side of my field because I didn't want it to interfere with my other crops. Soon, the plants grew taller than my head. When I felt that the stalks were ready to harvest, I cut them down and put them in the root cellar under the house.

I remembered that the stranger had told me that he smoked the Mary-Juanita so I figured that if you could smoke it, then you could also chew it. I got in the habit of coming to the house for dinner, and then going to the root cellar to chew some Mary-Juanita. After that, I would sometimes just sit on the porch and listen to the butterflies sing. Before I started using Mary-Juanita, I didn't know butterflies could sing. I called the stuff my "wacky tobaccy." Sometimes, I didn't even go back to the field after dinner. I just sat on the porch and relaxed.

A bad thing happened about two weeks after I started using Mary-Juanita. My missus began to notice that I was spending a lot of time in the root cellar and she wanted to know why. I decided to tell her about the stuff because I didn't think she would understand if I told her I was in the cellar with Mary-Juanita. I told her that the plants were a spice, kind of like sage, that you used to flavor food. I guess that is where my troubles and the troubles at the church really began. The next day when I came home for dinner, my wife had a wonderful meal cooked. I noticed that the food tasted a little different and so she said, "Guess what I cooked that with?" But I didn't have to guess. I knew that it was my Mary-Juanita. I began to eat some mighty fine meals in those days. Each day, there would be a new dish with her "spice" thrown in. Some of my friends commented that I was gaining weight, but I was ashamed to tell them that I was eating more and working in the fields less.

Some women just can't keep a secret, and my missus is one of them. She shared with the ladies of the Missionary Circle at church that she had discovered a new ingredient to flavor food, and that their husbands would really love it. Naturally, they all wanted to try it. Soon most of the families of the First Community Fellowship Church were cooking with Mary-Juanita on a regular basis. This might have been okay had it not been for the annual homecoming services with singing and dinner on the grounds.

The homecoming services were an all-day affair. First, Pastor Laster would conduct the morning service with a sermon and special singing. Then, the congregation would have the dinner in the church social hall. Each family would pitch in and bring a well-filled basket. After dinner, everyone would go back to the sanctuary for another round of preaching and singing. A few ladies would volunteer to warm up the dishes before the dinner began. On this particular day, the problem was that these were no ordinary dishes. Almost everything was heavily-laden with Mary-Juanita. As the food was warmed, the social hall began to be filled with the aroma of Mary-Juanita, and everyone began to feel a little giddy. Everyone had plenty to eat and many returned for second helpings. The fried chicken received rave reviews. Of course, it had a secret ingredient in it that even Colonel Sanders didn't know about. One lady brought a dish that looked like turnip greens. It was later determined that it was just Mary-Juanita straight.

After the delicious meal, everyone waddled back to the sanctuary for the afternoon worship service. The singing was something really beautiful with all those butterflies joining in. Then Pastor Laster, who had participated very heavily in the dinner activities, got up to preach. The pastor said, "I think that next year we should call this event the Ham and Yam Jam. Now I will take my text from the Gospel of John where Jesus said, "He that is without sin among you, let him first cast a stone at her.""

At this point, a man named Ed Jenkins stood up and said, "Pastor Laster, if we are going to cast stones out of our congregation, I feel that we ought to cast Ralph Stone out. He doesn't come much anyway, and he always messes up our men's Sunday School class attendance record." Pastor Laster finally got Ed settled down and was able to continue with his sermon. However, I think about half of the church were in favor of Ed's suggestion.

Pastor Laster delivered one of the best sermons that I've ever heard, although he got a little wound up and seemed to get some of his Bible facts mixed up. I always thought there were just the Ten Commandments and not twelve. I also thought there were twelve disciples and not ten. And that part about Samson killing the Philistines with the jawbone of a donkey – I have read that in the Scriptures, but I never read where he beat the living daylights out of them. Perhaps Pastor Laster was using one of those newer translations.

Well, the service finally ended, and everyone was ready to go home. The whole congregation agreed on one thing. Nobody knew who Mary-Juanita was, but they all said she must have been a mighty fine cook.

One sad thing happened concerning the Mary-Juanita usage. (Maybe this was a good thing.) I got so caught up in enjoying Mary-Juanita that I forgot to save any seeds. Those ladies down at the church used so much of it that we ran out. I bet it was the first time in the history of Christianity that the sin of greed helped keep a church on the straight and narrow. Most of the folks agreed, anyway, that it was fun to have a nice time, but it was even better to be able to remember it the next day.

"Hey there, Cool Daddy. Could I trouble you for a glass of water?"

Pastor Laster and the Revival Preacher

Rev. A.T. Laster sat in front of his fireplace with his friend and colleague, Rev. Martin Jacobs. It was late March and the two were sitting close to the fire. March weather is very unpredictable. Some days are warm and sunny, giving folks a sense of spring fever. Other days are cold and windy. The latter was the case on this particular day, with the temperature hanging in the middle twenties.

Rev. Laster was the pastor of the First Community Fellowship Church. It was a rural church, but it was one of the largest in the area. It was located about three miles south of Groveville, the capital city of Aardvark County. The congregation was not affluent, but rather they were a collection of farmers and other working people who, for years, had seen fit to be a part of that fellowship. Pastor Laster had been the shepherd of that flock for almost ten years. He was fresh out of seminary when he became the church's pastor. His first day as pastor, in his opinion, had been a disaster. Not only was he inexperienced in Biblical teaching and preaching, but also not yet fully developed his pastoral people relations skills.

On that first day, as he sat on the platform prior to the beginning of the morning worship service, he noticed an elderly man entering the sanctuary accompanied by a large dog. The man walked down the aisle and sat down on the third pew from the front on the left side. The dog lay down at his feet. Pastor Laster, still green in the ministry, thought that this should not be happening in the house of the Lord, so he stepped down from the platform and walked over to the man in question. Respectfully, he said to the man, "Sir, I really don't think that you should have that dog in here." So the man took the dog outside and returned to his seat just in time for the opening hymn.

When his time came, Pastor Laster made a valiant effort to preach his sermon. However, his nerves and the dog situation had left him rattled. This sermon was not one of his better efforts. After the final hymn was sung and the congregation was dismissed, the chairman of the deacons approached him. He said, "Preacher, I think that you may have offended John Loutin by asking him to take his dog out. You see, that dog has been coming with him for years and has never caused any problems, so we have allowed him to bring the dog with him. Besides that, John gives his tithe regularly, and we don't want to see him quit coming."

Pastor Laster then approached Mr. Loutin and said to him, "Brother, I didn't know the whole story about your dog, so I am very sorry that I asked you to take him out."

The old man looked at him and said, "That's all right, Preacher, it all worked out for the best. I don't reckon I'd want my dog to hear a sermon like that anyway."

There had been other mistakes like that, but the church had been very forgiving. With much prayer and patience,

Pastor Laster began to lead the church, and the congregation grew. There had been many good times at the church, as well as some heartaches and sorrows. The pastor was there through it all, to marry the young, bury the dead, and generally care for the flock.

It was a tradition at the First Community Fellowship Church that they have two revival services each year. You would think, according to some members of the church, that when God gave Moses the Ten Commandments on Mount Sinai, that he also chiseled into a third tablet of stone commanding the church to have the two yearly services. The church pastor would invite a guest preacher for the week of nightly meetings. The pastor also arranged for the guest preacher's lodging and meals. Pastor Laster had often allowed the preacher to lodge and eat meals with him for the week. This was the case with the Rev. Martin Jacobs.

As brothers Jacobs and Laster sat in front of the fire on this cold March night, they talked about the revival services that had gone on at the church that week. The Rev. Jacobs was a good speaker, and the folks had been eager to listen. He had closed out the meetings that very evening with a tremendous sermon on the torments of hell. Several people had made decisions to live closer to the Lord, and many folks who hadn't made public decisions went home and wished they had.

This was the last night that the Rev. Jacobs would be the guest of Pastor Laster. Those folks who have ever had to depend on a fireplace as the sole source of heat, know the importance of sitting close to the fireplace. As the fire burned brighter, the two preachers discussed the evening's sermon and what they thought hell would really be like.

Over in the corner of the room sat Matthew Laster, shivering. Matthew was the seven- year-old son of the Rev. Laster. He was a polite kid who was extremely wise beyond his years. At a lull in the conversation, the Rev. Jacobs saw Matthew in the corner and tried to draw him into the conversation. "Well Matthew," the preacher asked, "what do you think hell will be like?"

"I don't know, sir," replied the boy, "but I hope it's not like it is here."

Startled, Pastor Laster asked him, "What do you mean, Son?"

Matthew replied, "Well, here it is hard to get to the fire for all the preachers."

The New Bathroom

The First Community Fellowship Church had not always gone by that name. When the church was founded, it had been called Fellowship Baptist Church. The other Baptist church in the area was the Groveville Baptist Church, or the "town church," as it was sometimes called. After the church had been in existence for about thirty years, the congregation decided to change the name to Community Fellowship Church. The "Baptist" part was dropped because they felt that people from other denominations would feel more comfortable worshipping there. So, the Community Fellowship Church opened its doors to all Christians as long as they had been baptized properly by immersion, or "dunking," as some folks called it. Later, when Groveville Baptist Church became the First Baptist Church of Groveville, the church once more changed its name to First Community Fellowship Church.

The church was started in 1936 when America was trying to recover from the Great Depression. The first pastor was the Rev. B.O. Bass. People used to kid him and say that B.O. stood for "Big Old," as in Big Old Bass. Actually, though, his Christian name was Bradley Oliver Bass. Pastor Bass led the congregation in the construction of their first church building. Nobody had much money

13

in 1936, so they built a simple wood frame building with no running water. About fifty yards behind the church was Duncan Creek. Some of the people in that area thought it was spelled "Dunkin' Creek" because that is where Pastor Bass did the baptizing. Also behind the church, near the creek bank, but downstream from the baptizing hole, stood the church outhouse.

The church grew steadily under the shepherding of Pastor Bass. About six years after the church was started, a dear old saint died and left the church a thousand dollars in his will. A thousand dollars was a lot of money in those days. The people were excited about his benevolence, and everyone had an opinion about how it should be spent.

On the third Sunday in November, in 1942, a special business meeting was called to discuss the spending of the church's new windfall. At the meeting, Mr. Henry James stood up and said, "I think we should take the money and buy a chandelier like the town church has."

At this point, Mrs. Bertha Jackson, Ben Jackson's wife, rose and said, "I feel that we cannot buy a chandelier for three reasons. First of all, nobody knows how to spell it, so we can't order it. Secondly, if we could spell and order it, nobody would know how to play it. Thirdly, what we really need is more lights in here."

Lots of people agreed with Bertha, so the chandelier recommendation was voted down. After much discussion, the church decided that what they needed was running water, including the installation of a bathroom. Later, if there was money left over, they could add a baptistery. This campaign was actually led by the ladies. They stated that it was cold going outside to the outhouse, especially with dresses on. Another argument was that the outhouse cut down on the church fellowship, because no one wanted to shake hands with people after they went to the outhouse. Besides this, everyone agreed that it was mighty inconvenient in the winter, when the door was either snowed open or shut.

Soon the running water was piped in, and the bathroom project got under way. During the construction, several folks thought that Pastor Bass should hold a dedication service for the new facility once it was completed. He had never seen a dedication service for a bathroom, so he had no idea what kind of prayer would be appropriate. He searched for weeks through many prayer books and pastor's manuals, but could find nothing. So, when the dedication day finally came, this is what he prayed:

"Our Father, as we are here today to dedicate this facility, I pray that we would first of all, dedicate ourselves to you. We pray that a greater love for you would be installed in our lives. Sink into us the reality that our lives need to shine for you. May our love for you always run hot, and not lukewarm or cold. We also pray that all sin would be flushed from the chambers of our hearts.

"As we stand in line to partake of this blessing, help us to learn patience, consideration, strength, endurance, and love for our fellow man. May this movement lift the lid on our desire to bless others as you have blessed us. When we think of this facility, may it bring restoration when we feel drained; may it bring help when we are troubled; may it bring freedom when we are bound; may it bring peace when our insides are in turmoil. And Lord, may our sounds of joy echo through this chamber, and through the hallways of our church forever. Amen."

First Community Fellowship Church in its earlier days

George Washington
and the Hand Grenade

After the Fellowship Baptist Church got the new bathroom, things seemed to flow smoothly for a while. There was one man, however, who refused to use the new facility. He was a hillbilly at heart, so he felt that the call of nature should be answered outside, as close to nature as possible. The man's name was John Henry Slatton. The congregation sympathized with John Henry's feelings, but they felt that the best thing to do would be to destroy the outhouse.

Before the church decided to build the new bathroom, the outhouse had been the victim of a Halloween joke. On the previous Halloween, which was on a Saturday, the church held a party that night for the youth. Some of the older boys of the church, including Billy Bass, the fifteen-year-old son of the pastor, thought it would be funny to push the outhouse over into the creek. The plan was this: they would wait until the party was over; then, they would quickly push the outhouse over, and then, run like crazy. No one would discover the deed until Sunday morning.

Now, an outhouse was constructed so that the wood frame part of the building sat over a platform made of either concrete or wood, which covered the pit. Attached to this platform was the seat, which was a box-like structure, also made out of either wood or concrete. So, when the boys planned to push it over in the creek, they knew that they were only talking about the actual house, not the platform and seat.

The plan was put into play. With a mighty heave-ho, the outhouse went over just as planned. However, something went dreadfully wrong. Just as the outhouse hit the water, they heard a shout and realized that it had been occupied. At this point, the boys followed through with the last part of their plan and ran like crazy. In the darkness, they could not identify the victim and hoped the victim could not identify them. They went on home as if nothing had happened, but they went with fear and trembling.

Billy Bass knew he was going to be in trouble. He had always learned that it was good to be honest and to tell the truth. He had studied in school the story of George Washington and how he admitted to his father that he was the one who cut down the cherry tree. About an hour later, when his father came home, he asked Billy, "Son, did you have anything to do with pushing that outhouse over?"

Billy then responded, "Dad, I'm going to be like George Washington. I cannot tell you a lie. I did it." No sooner had the words left Billy's mouth, than Pastor Bass had his belt off and gave Billy a severe whipping. After a while, when Billy's bottom quit burning, he came to his father and asked him, "Dad, why did you whip me? I told you that I was going to be honest and wasn't going to tell you a lie."

The pastor replied, "The answer is simple, Son. When George Washington cut down the cherry tree, his daddy wasn't sitting in it."

All this was still fresh in the congregation's mind when they were discussing what do about the old outhouse. One Sunday in February of 1943, the folks were surprised, just before the morning service, to see young Stanley Anderson arrive at the church, wearing his new Army dress uniform. Stanley was the son of Herman and Myrtle Anderson who owned a farm nearby. He had just finished his basic training at Fort Jackson, in Columbia, South Carolina, and was on a two-week furlough before he went overseas to fight the Japanese. He had taken a bus from Columbia to Aardvark County and caught a ride to the church. He figured his parents would be there, so he decided to surprise them. Everyone was really excited to see him and filled him in on all the latest happenings.

After the service, Stanley heard the discussion about the outhouse. Stanley felt that he had an answer to the problem. He had obtained permission from his commanding officer to bring home three hand grenades. He wanted to help his father get rid of a couple of oak stumps on some land that he was clearing. He assured Pastor Bass and the deacons that he could solve the problem that very day with one grenade. Then, the next day, the men could get together and clean up the debris. Everyone got caught up in the excitement and agreed that they should do this immediately, while they had a grenade expert in their midst.

Stanley took a grenade out of his bag and walked around to the back of the church. In the excitement, no one noticed that one person was now missing from the mob that was assembling at the back corner of the church. That person was John Henry Slatton. Stanley pulled the pin from the grenade and tried to throw it the fifty yards to the outhouse. However, the grenade fell a little short. Looking back, this was a good thing. The grenade exploded and blew the outhouse all to pieces. The roof was on the other side of the creek, while the rest of it was a pile of kindling scattered across the ground. Also scattered around were pages from Sears and Roebuck catalogs. These catalogs solved the tissue issue when times were tough.

All that was left standing of the outhouse was the cement platform and seat. When the smoke cleared and the debris quit raining down from the sky, the people saw John Henry running up to the church, adjusting his Sunday suit trousers as he went. He ran up to Pastor Bass and shouted, "Preacher, I'm so sorry. I've learned my lesson though. I'll never try to light my pipe in one of those things again!" John Henry never did find his glasses, his hat, or his pipe, which is just as well because he decided to quit smoking anyway.

The grenade fell a little short. Looking back, this was a good thing.

The Education Drawback

Way back in 1930, a man named Sammy Woodford left Aardvark County and moved up north to Pittsburgh, Pennsylvania. The country was in the throes of the Great Depression, so he figured he would have a better opportunity for employment and survival if he moved there. He soon found himself in the big city, along with thousands of other people seeking employment and assistance. Sammy heard on the street that the Emmanuel Baptist Church, which was a fairly large congregation, needed a janitor immediately. When Sammy first saw the church building, he was amazed at how big it was, but he felt that he would be able to do the work. Sammy had one drawback, though. That was the fact that he could not read or write.

When Sammy applied for the job, the church office manager gave him an application to fill out. When Sammy explained that he couldn't read or write, the office manager said to him. "Mr. Woodford, this is a large and prestigious church. We have been in this community for over a hundred years, and many well-known society people attend here. I really don't feel that a man with your limited education would be a proper fit for a church of this caliber. I appreciate your interest, but I don't think we will be able to hire you." As Sammy was leaving the church, the office manager gave him two apples from the mission food box and wished him well.

At that time, the price of apples in some places on the street was two for a nickel. Sammy ate one of the apples because he was hungry. Then he thought to himself – I bet if I saved this other apple, then somebody will come along and give me a nickel for it. So, that's exactly what happened. Sammy sold his apple for a nickel. Then, he took that nickel and bought two more apples. When he sold them, he had a dime, which he used to buy four apples. After about a week of doing this, Sammy realized that he had started a business and that he was making money. Occasionally, Sammy had to eat an apple, but for the most part, he was doubling his money.

After about a month of selling apples, Sammy had enough money to purchase a push cart. Each day, he would be out on the street pushing his cart and building up his customer base. He diversified and added oranges and bananas to his inventory. He also learned where to buy wholesale at the best prices, for the most profit.

For two years, Sammy pushed that fruit cart up and down the streets of Pittsburgh. He had many customers who patronized his business on a regular basis. One day, the people who ran a produce shed where Sammy bought a lot of his items at wholesale, announced that they were retiring and offered to sell their business to Sammy. After much thought, Sammy decided to take the plunge and buy the place. He became the proud owner of Sammy's Quality Produce. Along with the building, he also took possession of an old truck that the previous owners had used. He promptly had his logo painted on the truck's doors.

For some reason, Sammy continued to prosper. He really worked hard to make his business successful, and his hard work paid off. Sammy knew the struggles of poor folks who were trying to make it in a bad economy. He was determined that he was not going to be hungry again. This was his motivation that kept him working, day after day, selling his wares.

After five years of working in the produce shed, Sammy took advantage of another opportunity and bought a produce warehouse. This was a big business for a country boy from Aardvark County. At the warehouse, the big trucks would come in and unload, and Sammy would fill orders to other dealers at wholesale prices. He continued to run his produce shed, where he sold to his long-time loyal customers. By this time, Sammy not only was busy himself, but he had thirty full-time employees. Sammy, through the years, had become prosperous and had built for himself a reputation as a hard-working, honest businessman. The nickel apple business had grown beyond his wildest dreams.

In 1940, as America was recovering from the Depression, banks began to regain the trust of the people. At this time, Sammy felt the need once again to expand his business. He went to the local bank to try to borrow fifty thousand dollars. The bank president knew of Sammy and his reputation for running a successful business. He told Sammy, "Mr. Woodford, our bank would be proud to loan you the money. Just fill out this little application as a formality, and we'll process your loan."

"But sir," Sammy replied, "I can't read or write."

The banker exclaimed, "You can't read or write? Wow! With all that money you've made, just imagine where you would be today if you could read and write."

"Sir," said Sammy, "I know where I'd be. I'd be the janitor at Emmanuel Baptist Church."

A Childhood Memory
from The Old-Timer

When I was a young'un back in the second grade, there was a student named Jim who was really tough. The teacher asked him, "Jim, if you had six apples and your neighbor took three of them, what would you have?"

Tough Jim replied, "I'd have a dead neighbor and all six of my apples."

The Two Sisters

Sally and Sadie Alverson were twin sisters who had grown up on a farm in Aardvark County. Their father had no sons, so the girls had been raised to help out with the farm chores, as well as perform the household duties. Their mother had died when they were ten years old, so the primary tasks of cleaning, cooking, and washing clothes fell to them. In their teen years, when they weren't in school, they spent their time working the fields and doing housework. Because of this, they had little time for socializing with the boys. This kind of life was hard and unfair, but it was useless to complain.

When the sisters were in their mid-twenties, their father died suddenly, leaving them the farm. After about two months of trying to run the farm themselves, the ladies realized that this was an impossible task. They then sold the farm and bought a small house in Groveville. Both of the women found jobs in town – Sally, as a floor walker in Hudson's 5&10, and Sadie, as a cook in the town's elementary school. The year was 1962, and things looked promising for the women.

When they lived on the farm, the sisters had washed their clothes in a #3 tin tub. This was back breaking work, as the clothes had to be washed, scrubbed, rinsed, and hung out to dry. They had brought their tub with them because they just naturally assumed that all people used them. Shortly after their arrival in town, they saw a sign in a window in a building next to the 5&10 that read Sparkle Clean Coin Laundry. They figured that as long as they were living in town, they might as well do as the towns folks did. So, the next day, the ladies brought all their dirty clothes to the coin laundry.

Being raised on the farm, the women had been sheltered from some of the nation's civil unrest. Things were happening across the South that was causing much turmoil. Race riots were commonplace across the nation. Sally and Sadie knew little of what all this meant. To them, people were just people, no matter what color their skin was. Having been raised outside the city, they knew nothing about the fact that different races had different facilities– different restaurants, different churches, different barber shops, and even different waiting rooms in doctor's offices.

All of this came into play when the ladies visited the coin laundry. They were new at this and really didn't know what they were doing. They also didn't know what the sign meant that read White Only! They were ignorant about the sign, they certainly didn't want to break any rules, so they washed their underwear, sheets, and pillowcases at the laundry and took their colored clothes home to be washed in the #3 tin tub. The next day, they went to Harry's Hardware and Appliances and bought themselves a washing machine. The ladies from the farm had arrived, big time.

The sisters settled into the routines of town living, and time passed by quickly. They made friends at work and church, but there was no romantic interest in either of their lives. Both sisters resented the fact that their teenage years had been spent on the farm where they were too busy to have boyfriends. Both of them felt that they were destined to be old maids.

As the years rolled by, and the sisters found themselves in their late thirties, their disposition toward men soured. In their minds, their opportunities for romance and marriage had passed. They viewed men as unnecessary animals. They had gotten along for almost twenty years without men in their lives, and they felt they had done just fine. The sisters had as their companion a cat that they named Cindy. The sisters' views on men were passed on to the cat, for Cindy was kept in the house at all times. Because of this, she entered the adult stage of cathood, also not ever having a boyfriend.

One day, Sally went shopping for groceries. As she came out of the door, carrying two bags, she accidently bumped into a man named Jeremy Green. Sally and Jeremy and the groceries went sprawling everywhere. Jeremy quickly got up, apologized for his clumsiness, and helped Sally collect her groceries. He then offered to walk Sally home and help her with the bags. Sally told him that she reckoned that would be okay. On the way home, she found out that Jeremy was new in town, having moved from Tennessee.

When they arrived at the house and he delivered the groceries to Sally, Jeremy asked her if, maybe, she would like to go out to dinner on Saturday night. He seemed like such an epitome of a charming, Southern gentleman, that Sally said that she reckoned that would be okay, too.

At the end of their dinner date, Jeremy asked if, maybe she would like to go out again. Sally reckoned that a second date would also be okay. Soon, her attitude toward men started to change. At least, her attitude toward one man in particular was changing. Sally didn't know exactly know how it happened, but after going out with Jeremy a few more times, she discovered that she was in love. After about three months of dating, Jeremy got down on one knee one evening and asked Sally to be his wife. Sally, the unclaimed blessing from the farm, reckoned that she would like that very much.

And so it was, that the following April, when the azaleas and the dogwoods were competing in nature's beauty contest, Sally walked down the church aisle and became the wife of Jeremy Green. After the wedding, the couple left for their honeymoon in New York City. A few days later, Sadie received a telegram from Sally. The message read: Having a great time in NYC. Let that cat out.

So, life turned out good for Sally Alverson Green. Life also turned out good for her sister. At Sally's wedding, Sadie met George, Jeremy's brother, who was an aspiring country music star. They struck up a relationship, and soon, Sadie and George took the plunge, got married, and set up housekeeping in Nashville.

Life also turned out good for Cindy, the other female in the house. After she was allowed to go out of the house on occasion, she met Tom, a handsome Persian from across the street, with whom she raised several offspring.

Gems of Wisdom
from The Old-Timer

If you have a kid who is not very good looking, do not let him play in the sandbox, especially if there are cats in the neighborhood. He might get covered up.

The Letter from Santa Claus

Joe Hanson owned a farm up in the northwest corner of Aardvark County. He was considered by many people to be a successful farmer and business man. Hard work had paid off for him – and for his wife and children. Through the years, the farm prospered, but in the beginning, Joe had struggled.

In 1961, Joe and his wife Nancy moved to Aardvark County to try their hand at farming. They had come from Pike County, Kentucky, where the main occupation was coal mining. With the help of a bank loan, Joe who was age twenty-eight at the time, bought a hundred-acre farm and moved to Aardvark County with his wife and their four-year old twins, Randy and Candy.

The first year went by okay, as Joe and Nancy adjusted to farm life. However, 1962 was a different story. A late freeze had damaged the apple trees which had just started to bloom. Also damaged was the pecan grove. Then, a summer drought had caused a tremendous decline in the vegetable production, as well as the other cash crops. Nancy took a part-time job as a substitute teacher to help out, and they were barely able to scrape together the bank payment for the land and equipment. They had food to eat, but little else as far as luxuries. The problem was that

Christmas was rapidly approaching, and the two children were looking forward to a visit from Santa Claus on Christmas Eve.

In early December, with the help of their mother, Randy and Candy wrote their letters to Santa with their wish lists. Candy asked for a new baby doll and crib. Randy wanted a "big-boy" size football. Both kids wanted new bicycles with training wheels. Neither Joe nor Nancy knew what to do. How could you tell a child that Santa might not visit this year? You couldn't tell them that Santa was sick or that he had died. Joe and Nancy firmly believed that you should never tell a child that Santa Claus was not going to visit because they had been bad. In their opinion, this promoted an idea of conditional love where the recipient had to prove that they were worthy of receiving favor. This went against their Christian upbringing. Besides all this, both children had been exceptionally good about doing their chores. Still, they were in a quandary about what to tell them. They tried to encourage their children, telling them to keep believing and things would work out for the best.

At supper on Christmas Eve, Randy and Candy were too excited to eat. They knew for sure that while they slept, Santa Claus would visit their house and leave them their toys. After the children were put to bed, Joe went to the barn to check on the animals and to think. As he stood in the barn, trying to mull things over in his mind, he realized that unless a miracle happened by morning, he would have to tell his children that Santa Claus had not come. Then, he bowed his head and simply said, "God, I need a miracle."

As Joe started to leave the barn he heard a whimper. Shining his flashlight over in the corner of a cow stall, he saw a stray dog huddled in the straw. The dog whimpered again. Upon closer examination, Joe found that the dog was a female mixed-breed who was giving birth to puppies. She had already given birth to one puppy, and as Joe watched, the second offspring was born. Joe gave her food and water and then left her alone.

Joe went inside and warmed himself by the fire. Suddenly a light went off in his brain that could have lit the entire county. Joe got a pen and paper and began to write a letter to his children.

The letter read:
Dear Randy and Candy,

I have chosen you to receive a special gift from me this year. I know that you wanted bikes and toys for Christmas, but I have a gift that is far better. In your barn, you will find two puppies—one for each of you. When I realized that these puppies needed a farm to run around on, I immediately thought of you. You can have bikes later, but this is a gift that needed to be given today.

This is a gift that you can love. This is also a gift that can love you back. Right now, the puppies can't see, but soon their eyes will be opened, and they will see you. One day, when you pick them up, they will lick your face and bring you great joy. Can a bicycle do that? I don't think so.

This is a gift that can give you companionship. You will always have someone to play with. Next year, when you go to school and the teacher tries to teach you things like spelling and reading, you have my permission to daydream, just a little, about your dog at home. When you get off that school bus, I'm sure your dog will be there to greet you with his tail wagging.

This is also a gift that teaches you responsibility because new puppies need care. They need to be fed and watered each day. They also need baths occasionally and need a warm home. This is one of the reasons why I chose you to receive this gift–I knew you could handle the responsibility.

Candy, because you are a girl, I know you will want to put ribbons on your puppy's ears and pretend she's a baby. Randy, I am sure you will enjoy teaching your puppy to chase a ball or fetch a stick. You will both like running the fields with them. So, kids, enjoy your puppies! Merry Christmas!

From:

Santa Claus

When they awoke the next morning, Candy and Randy were surprised to find an envelope with their names on it under the tree instead of toys. As their dad read the letter to them, they grew very excited. As soon as they were dressed, they hurried to the barn with their parents to see the new puppies. Candy's puppy was a reddish-brown color; she immediately named it "Angel." Randy's puppy was black with a white spot on his forehead. Randy named him "Star."

Amazingly, the mother dog did not mind that the children had interrupted the feeding time or that her babies had a red ribbon tied around them. No one ever knew where that dog came from, or why she suddenly disappeared shortly after the puppies were weaned. Years later, at Christmas family gathering, Joe, Nancy, Randy, and Candy agreed that their most memorable Christmas was the one in 1962 when once again, a miracle happened in a cow stall.

A Christmas Memory from The Old-Timer

When I was a kid, we were so poor that on Christmas Eve, my daddy took his shotgun out behind the barn, fired one shot, and came in and told us Santa Claus had committed suicide.

The Artist

Andy Smith was one of the most talented individuals in Aardvark County. His talent lay in the fact that he could paint just about anything. In a county where a lot of people thought that culture was the drinking of buttermilk, it was nice to know Andy's talent brought real culture to the area. Andy had painted several pictures which he had displayed at local shows in the county.

Everyone assumed that because Andy was talented with a paint brush, that he was also highly intellectual. This was a misconception. Even though he had graduated from Groveville High School, he was just an average student. In fact, his studies had often lagged, due to the fact that he spent his time in class drawing.

One person in particular who had a misconception about Andy's intellectual abilities was Wade Hampton Grove, the president of Groveville State Bank. Mr. Grove came from a prestigious family in Aardvark County. Not only was his family among the original settlers of the town, but also from an ancestral line of famous people. While doing research on his family tree, he discovered that he was distantly related to General George Armstrong Custer, the famous Indian fighter who lost his life at the battle of Little Big Horn. This really excited Mr. Grove, so he decided to have a picture painted depicting General Custer's last battle. He planned to have the wall-sized picture hung in the bank. Now, Mr. Grove had heard of Andy's artistic ability, so he contacted him about painting the picture. What he wanted, in particular, was for Andy to research General Custer and find out what his exact last words were. That way, the picture would capture the true emotions of the general just moments before his death. The bank president and Andy agreed on the price for the project and shook hands on the deal. Then, Andy began his research.

Andy was one of those artists who did not like suggestions from people when he was working on a project. For this reason, he refused to let anyone see any of his paintings until they were completely finished. His philosophy was this: Michelangelo did not ask for advice, so why should I? For two months, Andy labored over the painting. This would be his biggest project yet, and he wanted to be sure to do a good job. Finally, he called Mr. Grove and told him that the painting was done. The banker was excited, and so, they set a date for the great unveiling ceremony.

And so it came to pass, that on the last Saturday in April of 1979, the unveiling ceremony took place. Mr. Grove spared no expense for the ceremony. Everybody who was somebody in Aardvark County was invited. The mayor was in attendance, along with many local politicians and dignitaries. The high school band had been commissioned to play for the ceremony. Mr. Grove had also enlisted some of the fine ladies from his church to help serve refreshments.

On the speaker's platform sat the bank president, the mayor, the bank's board of directors, and Andy Smith, dressed in his Sunday suit. Under a canvas, was the precious picture of General Custer, having been seen by no one but Andy.

The mayor rose first and made a short speech, thanking Mr. Grove for his generosity in having the picture painted and giving it to the town to enjoy. He then expressed his anticipation of seeing the great painting. Then, Mr. Grove stood up and made his speech. He said, "Folks, as you know, I recently found out that I am related to General Custer. That is why I commissioned young Andy Smith here to paint this picture that will hang in our bank for all the town to see. What you will be seeing, is the emotion and passion on the face of General Custer as he spoke his last words. With that in mind, I present to you Mr. Andy Smith and his painting of General Custer's last words."

At that point, Andy stood up, took a bow, and removed the canvas from the painting. It is good that Mr. Grove had already made his speech because at this point, he was speechless. There was a brief stunned silence among the crowd, and then, a few snickers developed. Soon, just about everyone was doubled over in laughter. There, on the canvas was the beautiful painting of General Custer. In the upper right-hand corner was a picture of a cow wearing a halo. General Custer was there looking at Indians who were on the ground picking cotton.

When Mr. Grove regained his composure, he stammered, "What is the meaning of this, young man?"

"Well, sir," replied Andy, "these are the last words of

General Custer – 'Holy cow! Where did all these cotton-picking Indians come from?'"

"Holy Cow! Where did all these cotton-picking Indians come from?"

The Nude Painting

After Andy Smith painted the picture of General Custer's last stand, his popularity as an artist grew. Actually, he became a celebrity around town. He was hailed among the working class as the man who put one over on the elite. Mr. Wade Hampton Grove was the one who became known as the laughing stock of Aardvark County. When he passed people on the street, he was certain that he heard snickers behind his back. He also imagined that he saw sly smiles and winks when he was talking to folks. At one point, he considered not hanging the painting in the bank as he had promised, because he considered the whole project a fiasco. It was only when he was advised by his wife and others that his reputation as a man of integrity was at stake, did he relent and hang the picture. His wife kindly pointed out that, maybe, the town folks would not want to do business with a banker who did not honor his end of a bargain.

Mr. Grove compromised about hanging the painting in the bank. He hung it in the room where the safe-deposit boxes were located. That way, he honored his promise to hang the painting, and it wasn't available for everyone to see and laugh at. After a couple of months, when he got over his mad spell, he went to Andy privately and hired him to paint another picture of General Custer. This time, he was specific about what he wanted. There were to be no cows with halos or Indians picking cotton. This time, there would be no unveiling ceremony – no bands, no big speeches, no dignitaries, and certainly, no surprise endings. When Andy finished the painting, Mr. Grove hung it in the lobby of the bank where it stayed for many years.

Because everyone in Groveville knew about the paintings at the bank, Andy became more recognized as an artist, not only by the common man, but also by the upper echelons of society. Even though the original General Custer painting was funny, folks had to admit that Andy Smith was indeed a talented artist. Andy's painting caught the eye of Mrs. Patricia Panderhurst. She was a rich society lady who had been invited to the original unveiling ceremony. Her husband was Steven Panderhurst, the state senator. Mrs. Panderhurst, who was age thirty-five at the time, was a fairly nice looking woman. She worried, though, that as she got older, her beauty would fade and that her husband would find her less attractive. She decided she would like to have a portrait of herself painted as an anniversary present for him, so that he would always be able to remember her in the prime of her attractiveness. She made an appointment with Andy to discuss the painting.

Andy arrived at the Panderhurst house to discuss the portrait with Mrs. Panderhurst. She did not seem to balk at the price of one thousand dollars, and the deal was struck. When they made arrangements for the sitting, Mrs. Panderhurst gave Andy a surprise. She said to him, "Andy, there is just one more thing about the portrait. I would like for you to paint me in the nude."

Andy was temporarily at a loss for words. He had never done a portrait in the nude before. When he regained his composure, he said to her, "Mrs. Panderhurst, I do not do paintings in the nude. You will have to find yourself another artist."

Mrs. Panderhurst then responded to him. "Andy," she said, "I really want this portrait for my husband, and I want to have it done in the nude. I am willing to pay you two thousand dollars to do it."

Andy had never in his life made that kind of money, but he still had his Christian principles to uphold. He told her, "Ma'am, you don't understand. It's not about the money. I just do not do paintings in the nude."

Once again, Mrs. Panderhurst had a counter offer. "Andy, it's you who doesn't understand. I want this painting done in the nude so badly that I am willing to pay you three thousand dollars to do it."

The temptation of making three thousand dollars was too much for Andy and his Christian principles. He succumbed to the temptation. He told her, "Okay, Mrs. Panderhurst, I will do the portrait in the nude for three thousand dollars, but do you mind if I at least leave my socks on, so I will have somewhere to stick my extra brushes?"

Gems of Wisdom
from The Old-Timer

There are three stages of life for everybody. They are:
- Youth
- Middle Age
- You're looking good

Bubba's Bright Ideas

One of the most colorful characters in Aardvark County was a young man named Bubba Brunson. If bright ideas could be sold for a dollar apiece, Bubba would be a millionaire because he probably had thought of a million of them. In 1989, Bubba went to the picture show and saw the movie "Rain Man," starring Dustin Hoffman. This was a movie about a man who had to deal with a brother who was mentally challenged. Bubba was so impressed with this movie that he went to see it six times. It became his favorite movie of all time.

Bubba got to thinking that if someone could write a movie script and give it a simple title like "Rain Man," then maybe he could write a movie script too. So, Bubba thought for awhile and wrote a script about a plumber and called it simply, "Drain Man." He sent it to a Hollywood movie producer and sat back to dream of his fortune. A few weeks later, Bubba received a nice letter from the producer thanking him for sending the script, but also telling him that they would have to decline the submission at this time. It was the first of many rejection slips.

After this, Bubba really put his thinking cap on and came up with another movie idea. This story was about a

49

gas stove repairman. He called it "Propane Man" – and sent the script to Hollywood. Once more, he got a rejection slip. Bubba seemed to have a brain like concrete; it was all mixed up and permanently set. Bubba was not about to let two rejections hinder him from living the lifestyle of the rich and famous. After all, by this time, he had already been smitten by the writer's bug. Bubba realized that the Hollywood crowd probably wasn't interested in common workers like plumbers and repairmen, so he decided to write movies about professional people instead. After thinking for awhile, he came up with a story about a neurosurgeon. This one, he called "Brain Man." A few days after sending it to Hollywood, Bubba got another rejection letter. Not to be deterred, Bubba wrote another movie script about a dentist which he called "Pain Man." This idea also was rejected.

Perhaps the most popular of Bubba's movie ideas was the last one he wrote. Many of us folks in Aardvark County felt like this one would be successful. This one was a Tarzan movie. In this story, Bubba had Tarzan leaving the jungles of Africa to move to New York City. After moving to New York, he began to enjoy the social scene and soon developed the lifestyle of a cross-dresser. Bubba called this movie, "Jane Man." Once more, Bubba's idea was rejected.

After all of these rejections, Bubba was devastated. He had always been able to do a little shade-tree auto mechanic work, so he decided to go to Detroit and learn how to fix cars the right way. After moving up north, he enrolled in a Ford Motor mechanics training school and settled in to the rigors of academics mixed with hands-on instruction. After a couple of years of hard work, Bubba was the proud recipient of a diploma. After graduation, Bubba decided to return to Aardvark County to set up shop there. The only problem was that while in school, Bubba developed a severe case of "the big head." Now that he was a professional mechanic, he decided that he was only going to repair Ford cars. Not only that, but because he was now a "specialist," he was only going to operate on a particular kind of Ford compact car.

With that thought in mind, Bubba rented a garage, had a sign painted, and went into business for himself. He was promptly arrested and hauled into court before the magistrate for operating an illegal business. The judge asked Bubba some questions, and Bubba answered them as well as his knowledge would allow. Suddenly, it seemed like a light bulb went off in the judge's brain, and he began to grin. He then said to Bubba, "Mr. Brunson, as an American, I appreciate the fact that an individual, under the free enterprise system can start out with nothing and make a million dollars or more, if he so desires. I also appreciate the fact that you have tried to do just that. I admire you for your hard work in school and for your willingness to work here among the people of Aardvark County. But, Mr. Brunson, under no circumstances will we now, or ever, allow you to call your business, Bubba's Escort Service."

"Mr. Brunson, at no time will we here in Aardvark County allow you to call your business Bubba's Escort Service."

Arlene Brunson

Bubba Brunson had a sister named Arlene. Now, Arlene Brunson was not easy on the eyes. If you have ever heard the old adage, *Beauty is skin deep, but ugly goes to the bone; beauty will fade away, but ugly will just hang on,* then you would realize that this applied to Arlene, for it hung all over her. There are those who believe that there is no such thing as an ugly woman. If that statement is true, then surely Arlene Brunson just squeaked by the goalpost that was the boundary by which women's beauty was judged. When a baby is born, people will often come and say their "oohs" and "aahs" and comment on how cute the baby is. In Arlene's case, they came, they looked, and they reserved their comments for the privacy of their own homes.

Arlene started out in life being cosmetically challenged, and she never outgrew it. The people of Aardvark County were not particularly mean to her because of her looks. She knew what she looked like; everyone else knew it too, so they just accepted it and went on with their lives. As Arlene grew through her teen years and into adulthood, she had one obsessive thought. She wanted to get married and raise a family. This was her driving goal. One time, when Pastor Laster was going to perform a simple wedding ceremony for an elderly couple after the morning worship service, Arlene got really embarrassed. When the pastor said, "Those of you who want to get married come down to the altar," Arlene was on her feet and started down the aisle before she realized what the pastor had actually meant.

Once, when Arlene was about twenty-five, two of her friends decided to play a joke on her. They set Arlene up with a blind date. She had been on blind dates before, but no one had ever wanted to start a relationship with Arlene Brunson. The joke was this: Bob Scuttles, the blind date, was actually blind. Never had his eyes seen the light of day. So, when he showed up at Arlene's door, he brought with him Rex, his German shepherd seeing-eye dog. He was truly the "blind date."

Sometimes, even practical jokes backfire. This was the case in this situation, because Arlene and Bob seemed to hit it off. They began to date on a regular basis, and everything worked out fine. Arlene had a handsome boyfriend that she could show off around town, and Bob had a girlfriend that he could admire for her inner beauty, be it buried ever so deep. They fell in love, and after six months of dating, they decided to get married and spend the rest of their lives together. They were married at First Community Fellowship Church, with Pastor Laster officiating.

And so it was, that Arlene and Bob Scuttles settled down to married life, and everybody lived happily ever after. Well, almost everybody! After only two weeks of looking at Arlene Brunson Scuttles, the German shepherd seeing-eye dog, Rex, lapsed into a coma, and had to be put to sleep.

Gems of Wisdom
from The Old-Timer

If you want to see real beauty, get someone to hold a honey bee in his hands. Then look into his eyes. Everyone knows that beauty is in the eyes of the bee holder.

The Practical Joker

Bubba and Arlene Brunson had a cousin named William Smithers. William was known around Aardvark County as a practical joker. He loved to play jokes on people. The congregation of the First Community Fellowship Church was well aware of his antics. William had often showed up at church dinners with cement pies or wooden cakes. He enjoyed standing around and watching as the church ladies tried to cut that particular dessert. Everyone was so used to his shenanigans that often they couldn't tell if he was being serious or just joking when he talked.

Several years ago, there was a group of people who traveled around and tried to sell trinkets to support their families because they claimed to be deaf. These people would approach someone in a parking lot and hand them a card with a key ring attached to it. The message on the card would read: *I am deaf. I am selling these key rings to support my family. Please donate $1 to help with this cause. Thank you!* Whether these people were actually deaf or just scammers, no one knew. William felt that these people were con artists. He personally knew several people who were totally deaf, but they held full-time jobs. William had no way to prove that these people were cons; that is, until he came up with the perfect plan to put these folks in their place.

William had a card printed that he kept in his wallet for the next time that he encountered one of these "deaf people." A few weeks later, he was sitting in a parking lot waiting for his wife to finish shopping. He was approached once again by a "deaf" bearer of trinkets. When the man showed him his card, William retrieved his card and showed it to the salesman. William's card read: I CAN'T READ. The deaf man read William's card, shook his head, and walked on to find another customer.

At one time in his life, William played a practical joke that backfired and caused him bodily injury. He was working on his house, using a staple gun to put weather-stripping around his windows. When he was almost finished, he ran out of staples. He didn't have time to go buy more, because this was Wednesday night, and he was going with his family to the mid-week prayer service at the church. Suddenly, William had an idea for another joke. He went inside and informed his family that he had a new way to keep up his socks. They shrieked as he proceeded to fire the empty staple gun at his ankle. William laughed until he almost cried. He thought it was so funny that he took the gun with him to church and showed his friends how a real tough-man keeps his socks up. The church folks just shook their heads and smiled at the latest of William's tricks.

Like the biblical King Asa of Judah, William had trouble with his feet. He was a regular patient of Dr. Anthony Lamont, a noted podiatrist in Aardvark County.

It just so happened that he had an appointment with the doctor the next afternoon. William thought that it would just be hilarious if he showed Dr. Lamont his new joke with the staple gun. After the doctor examined William and redressed his foot, William pulled the staple gun from his coat pocket and said, "Look, Doc, I've found a new way to keep up my socks." William then pulled the trigger on the staple gun.

Did I mention that William had a brother named Sonny who liked to borrow his tools? Did I also mention that William gave him free-rein of his garage as long as he returned what he borrowed? Did I mention that on that very day, Sonny came by, and finding no one at home, borrowed the staple gun? Did I further mention that Sonny bought staples for it and that he returned it full? Perhaps, I should have mentioned it, because that is exactly what happened.

The smile very quickly left William's face and he yelled in pain. The staple gun shot a 9/16 inch staple into his leg just above the ankle. The blood began to flow freely down William's leg and foot. As he tried to help William, the good doctor wondered about the intelligence of someone who would pull such a stunt as this. An hour later, after performing an emergency "staple-ectomy," giving William a tetanus shot, and having his office floor mopped, Dr. Lamont was still not a happy camper. He informed William that he took his profession seriously and that he did not have time for clowns. He also told William that if something like that happened again, he would be shopping for a new foot doctor.

William, taken aback by the incident, made two important decisions that very day. He vowed never to allow Sonny to borrow his tools again and to never attempt another practical joke. To his credit, he kept these vows faithfully without backsliding for six months.

Special Announcement
from Pastor Laster

Those of you who are in the habit of putting buttons instead of quarters in the offering plate, please bring your own buttons from home. Do not take them out of the church pew cushions.

Trouble at the Church

William Smithers went to church faithfully. He and his family were there for most of the regular weekly services and for the special church events. His brother Sonny, however, was just the opposite. Sonny rarely went to church. He saw no need to congregate with the believers because he was not a believer. He actually believed that church was for children and older people. At this time in his life, he felt no need for organized religion. He spent a lot of his free time with some of his drinking buddies, having fun and carousing. Often, Sonny would come home to his wife Brenda with black eyes or with scrapes and bruises from the fights he had been in.

Brenda, unlike her husband Sonny, was a faithful church member. She had taught Sunday school for years and was a good church worker. When she would patch Sonny up after one of his fights, she felt that God was using her to be a godly influence in her husband's life. She prayed for him and continually tried to encourage him to go to church and turn from his evil ways. One Saturday evening, on one of those rare occasions when Sonny was totally sober, he informed Brenda that he was going to church the next day. Brenda was elated. Actually, Sonny was just trying to get her off his back for a while.

Unfortunately, on Sunday morning Brenda had a terrible headache and could not attend church. She cheerfully sent her husband off to church and told him how proud she was of him. Her elation was short-lived however, when a couple of hours later, Sonny came home with two black eyes. With tears in her eyes she told him, "I thought you promised me you were going to church, but here I see you went out with your friends again."

Sonny replied, "You don't understand! I did go to church."

Brenda then asked him, "Okay, Mister Smarty Pants, how did you get those shiners on your eyes?"

"Well," explained Sonny, "I was sitting in the pew, minding my own business, when a lady came in late and sat down in front of me. About that time, the music director asked us to stand and turn to page 337 in the hymnal. The song that we sung was called 'Rescue the Perishing.' When we stood up, I saw that in her haste, the lady in front of me had run her dress down in the top of her panty hose. I thought about the song we were singing, so I decided to rescue her. I reached out and pulled her dress out of its entrapment. At this point, she turned around and bopped me in the eye."

Brenda thought for a minute and then replied, "Well, I guess maybe something like that could actually happen." Then, she had another thought and said, "But, wait a minute. How did you get the other black eye?"

Her husband answered, "Well, I realized that I had made her mad, so I wanted to do what was right. The music director told us to stand and turn to page 152 in the hymnal. The name of that song was 'Take My Life and Let It Be.' When we were singing the song, I realized I should have let her dress be, so I stuck it back in her hose just like it was. This made her mad again, so she turned around and hit me in the other eye."

Brenda was infuriated. How could anyone be so crazy that they would do something like that in church? All that afternoon, she did not speak to Sonny. She tried to pray about the situation, but she could find no peace. Finally, just before bedtime, she spoke to Sonny and said, "Sonny, I feel that you acted like a jerk today, but as a Christian, I am willing to forgive you. I want to give you a warning, though. The next time you pull a stunt like that, my frying pan and I will make you sing the song 'Will There Be Any Stars In My Crown Tonight?'"

Out of the Mouths of Babes

Brenda Smithers was a faithful Sunday school teacher at First Community Fellowship Church. For years, she had taught a class of six to eight year olds. She really enjoyed this age group, as she felt she had an influence on their Christian development. Through the years, she had taken an active interest in the lives of her students. She and her husband Sonny had no children of their own, so she always considered each member of the class her "kids."

Brenda also had a repertoire of funny sayings that her kids had repeated down through the years. One of the most memorable was the time that the lesson was going to be about Moses crossing the Red Sea. She asked the question at the beginning of class, "Who can tell me about the crossing of the Red Sea?"

Johnny Laster, who was a first cousin of Matthew Laster and was visiting him for the weekend, raised his hand. When Brenda called on him, he began, "Well, as far as I can remember, after Moses led the people out of Egypt, he came to the Red Sea. The sea was huge, so there was no way around it. Moses did not know what to do. He knew that Pharaoh's army was right behind him. He was trapped, so he prayed and said, 'God, I don't know what you're going to do, but you'd better do it ASAP.' God answered

Moses's prayer and sent the Army Corps of Engineers down to the sea. They quickly built a pontoon bridge, and every last one of them walked over to the other side. When Pharaoh's army saw this they said, 'If those crazy Israelites can go over, so can we.' So the Egyptians started to cross the bridge too. Moses waited until all the Egyptians got on the bridge. Then, he took a hand grenade out of the pocket. He often carried a hand grenade in his robe for emergencies such as this. Moses pulled the pin from the grenade, threw it onto the bridge, and blew all the Egyptians to kingdom come."

Everyone had sat spellbound as Johnny told this story. When he was finished, Brenda asked, "Now, Johnny, did it really happen that way?"

Johnny replied, "No, Ma'am, but if I told you the real story, you wouldn't believe it."

Another time that something really funny happened, was one Sunday when the lesson was on the feeding of the five thousand. Brenda felt that because one of the characters in this story was the young boy who willingly gave his few fish and loaves to Jesus, her class would relate more fully to him. As she taught the class, she emphasized how the people were hungry and how they had stayed all day listening to the teachings of Jesus. She also emphasized that, like that small boy, Jesus could use anything that was given freely to Him. She then asked the question, "What would you have brought to Jesus that day to help take care of that crowd?"

Cindy Wilson responded to the question by saying, "I would have brought enough pizza to feed everybody."

Then Darlene Smithers, who was William and Susan's daughter and Brenda's niece, spoke up and said, "I think I would have stopped by the store and bought enough Cokes and Oreos for everyone."

Then Brenda asked, "Does anyone else have an answer?"

Matthew Laster, the preacher's kid, who always seemed to come up with gems of wisdom, said, "If I had been going to hear Jesus preach that day, I would have taken an old car door with me."

Puzzled, Brenda asked him, "Matthew, why in the world would you want to carry a car door with you?"

Matthew gave her a look that seemed to say—How could you be a teacher and not know this? Then, he replied, "Don't you know that if we had a car door and it got hot, then we could roll the window down?"

Sometimes children say things that are funny, but at other times, from their mouths comes profound wisdom. One day, just before Brenda was going to dismiss the class with prayer, Darlene asked, "May we pray for Uncle Sonny?" Sonny, her husband, was a liquor-drinking, hard-living, carousing gambler, who very much needed their prayers.

That day at lunch, Brenda told her husband, "Darlene asked us to pray for you today and we did." Sonny said nothing but went into the living room to watch TV.

The next week at a family gathering, Darlene told her uncle, "Uncle Sonny, we prayed for you in church last week. Why don't you ever come to church?" Sonny didn't have an answer, but all week, he thought about that question.

When Sunday rolled around, he went with Brenda to church, but not before telling her that he was perfectly happy with his lifestyle and that he had no intention of changing his ways. At the church, Darlene asked her parents for permission to sit with Sonny and Brenda. Sonny got through the sermon okay; he had heard sermons before, and they did not seem to have any effect on him. After the sermon, the pastor extended as invitation for those who wanted to receive Christ as their Savior to come forward as they were singing the closing hymn. Sonny started to sing the hymn, but he couldn't seem to concentrate. He looked down and saw the blue eyes of his little blond–haired niece looking back at him. He tried to sing once more, but again, he saw his niece looking up at him. After that, he couldn't see very clearly, for tears welled up in his eyes. Sonny stepped out into the aisle and walked to the front of the church. Pastor Laster greeted him at the altar, and together, they knelt at the altar and Sonny received Jesus as his Savior.

The next week, Sonny was baptized into the fellowship of the church, where he became a faithful member. From the day of his conversion forward, he carried a picture of his little niece, Darlene, in his wallet. When times got rough for him, he would pull out that picture and be reminded of what God had done for him and how the words of a child had caused him to enjoy the blessings of God.

Special Announcement
from Pastor Laster

This announcement concerns our children's movie night. Due to technical difficulties, "The Invisible Man" will not be seen this week.

The World's Oldest Profession

According to movie writers and producers in Hollywood, the world's oldest profession is the selling of sinful physical pleasures. These producers and writers are wrong. The world's oldest profession is farming. Way back in the Garden of Eden, God told Adam that he would till the land to grow crops and that thorns and thistles would grow up in the land. Adam was also told that by the sweat of his face, he would work.

Today, farmers are still trying to fight the thorns and thistles, along with crabgrass and other weeds that plague them. There are many new inventions and techniques that have been developed to make farming easier, but still it is a hard life. The farmer is at the mercy of the weather and other factors that determine his success. For the full-time farmer, that means that often, he is up before the sunrise and works until dark. There are no sick days when he can stay out of work. There are also no paid vacations. It is often a thankless job. Everything that we have on our plates at mealtime, with the exception of fish, is produced by a farmer somewhere. Even the hamburgers that we so often enjoy were produced in their entirety by a farmer. People often bow their heads to give thanks to God for the provision of their food. Perhaps, it would also be appropriate to ask God to continue to bless the farmers, because without them, the whole world would starve.

Why then does the farmer put up with such difficulties in order to survive? Most farmers would probably say that they actually enjoy their work. It seems that working the soil gets in their blood, and they wouldn't be happy doing anything else. The farmer depends on his farm for his family's economic survival. That is why Farmer Colin Brown was concerned about his declining cow herd population. Mr. Brown had a herd of about fifty Hereford cows, which he raised in addition to growing crops. The raising of cattle was something that he could depend on for income, even when the crops failed.

Mr. Brown had noticed that his cows were not calving as often as they should. The trouble was traced back to Otto, his prize bull. We don't really need a biology class review to realize that the work of a bull is a necessary public service for the procreation of the cow family. It seemed that Otto, that sixteen hundred pounds of prime beef, had suddenly become uninterested in the "public service department." He seemed to pay no attention to the cows whatsoever. Mr. Brown had no choice but to call Dr. Abercrombie, one of the most qualified veterinarians in Aardvark County.

Dr. Abercrombie had a thriving farm animal practice, along with his work with small animals. His specialty was working with dogs and cats. He offered a free service for senior citizens if they chose to have their pet spayed or neutered. Once, he answered his phone to hear a lady ask, "Are you the doctor that gives neutering to senior citizens?"

When he assured her that he was that doctor she said, "Good, I'll send my husband right over." A few seconds later, she called back and told the doctor, "I mean I'll send my husband over with our dog."

When he received Mr. Brown's call about Otto, he hurried out to the farm. Otto was standing off in the corner of the pasture all by himself. He paid no attention to the nice-looking cows who wandered by from time to time. The doctor diagnosed Otto's ailment and gave the farmer a bar of medicine. His instructions were to break off a piece of it and feed it to Otto until it was gone. He assured Farmer Brown that Otto would soon be back to normal and feeling like himself.

After about a week, the medicine was all gone and so were Otto's troubles. Otto was happy again and so were the cows and Mr. Brown. A few days later, he was talking to his neighbor and singing the praises of Dr. Abercrombie and that miracle medicine. The neighbor then asked him, "What kind of medicine was that?"

Mr. Brown replied, "I don't know, but it tastes kind of like licorice."

Pastor Laster's
Favorite Sermon Illustration

A hog and a chicken go into a restaurant for breakfast. Both of them decide that they want ham and eggs. The waiter takes their order but returns to their table a short time later. He tells the hog and chicken, "I'm sorry but we are all out of ham and eggs." Then he has an idea and says, "Hey, wait a minute. I can get some ham from you, Mr. Hog, and some eggs from you, Miss Hen, and we can cook them so you can have ham and eggs."

The chicken replies, "Okay let's do that."

The hog then says, "Wait a minute, lady. For you that is just a contribution, but for me it's a total commitment."

Mary Alice's Streak of Luck

In the 1970s, a fad developed among college kids that was called "streaking." Streaking was just a fancy was of saying that someone was running naked. All across America, on college campuses and in a lot of other places, people were losing their inhibitions (and their clothes) and running around airing their differences. Streakers were turning up everywhere–in college cafeterias, classrooms, sports events, and sometimes, even at graduation exercises. Some schools made rules that if any potential graduate did not remain fully clothed during the ceremonies, they would not receive their diplomas. The fad became so popular, it was rumored that even at a well known, straight-laced Bible college, in the Deep South, two students were caught streaking. What had happened in that situation was this: a male student took off his tie, and a female student pulled her dress up to her knees. Together, they ran across the parking lot by the school's administration building.

Because of the widespread news coverage of college student's streaking activities, most of America missed the fact that there were other groups of people streaking too. It is a little known fact that there were occasional reports of senior citizens' streaking. One of these reports came from Aardvark County. At the Sunshine Home, an assisted living facility in Groveville, there lived two elderly female residents who had been lifelong friends. Their names were Mary Alice and Lucille. These ladies had heard about the streaking fad among the youth and wondered why it always seemed that young people got to have the most fun. The ladies had always been adventurous, and each would do anything on a dare.

One day at the lunch table, the talk was about the reports of streaking on the news. One of the other residents turned to Mary Alice and Lucille and said, "I dare you two to go streaking this afternoon." Well, the challenge had been issued – the gauntlet had been thrown down. That afternoon, the two ladies poked their heads out the door of their rooms and saw no one in the hallway. Then suddenly, here they went, fully naked down the hallway. Unfortunately, their escapade was noticed by an administration lady, who later admonished them that nice ladies did not do such things. It was just a short trip down the hallway and back, but the thrill and exhilaration of what they had done had them hooked.

About a week later, the two ladies got a little bolder. They knew what the office lady had said, but they had been smitten by the streaking bug. This time they went a little further. They ran naked down the hallway, across the front visiting room, out the front door, and across the front porch. Sitting at a table playing checkers, were two of the male residents of Sunshine Home. As the two ladies ran by, one of the men asked the other, "What was that lady wearing?"

"I don't know," said his friend, "but she needs to go back and iron it."

A few weeks later Mary Alice and Lucille were sitting on the porch of Sunshine Home. This time, they were fully clothed. Across the street was Happy Mary's Flowers and Gifts. Lucille turned to her friend and said, "I double-dog dare you to go streaking through that flower shop." Mary Alice really didn't want to, but she had been double-dog dared. Her reputation was at stake. So, off went her clothes, and off she went, running across the street.

Mary Alice returned in about five minutes with a bouquet and a blue ribbon. "Where did you get those things?" asked Lucille.

"Well," said her friend, "I won this for having the best dried arrangement."

Christian Kindness at the Barbershop

Clarence Green and his wife Annabelle lived above his barber shop in an apartment. The Greens were fairly newcomers to Aardvark County, having only been there five years. Clarence (a.k.a. Shorty) and Annabelle attended the First Community Fellowship Church where Pastor Laster preached, even though they lived closer to the First Baptist Church of Groveville. Both of the Greens were active in church and community affairs. Each of them was known as a dedicated Christian. In fact, someone commented to Annabelle one day that they often heard on the street the sound of her singing hymns, coming from their apartment in the mornings. This person loved the concert, but was curious as to why she only sang "The Old Rugged Cross" each day. Annabelle replied, "The answer is simple; that song is my egg timer. I sing three verses for soft-boiled eggs and five verses for the hard-boiled ones."

When Shorty first came to Groveville, he tried his best to show kindness to his fellow man. He was always especially kind to preachers, because his father had been a preacher back up in the hills of Tennessee. He had a habit of offering a free first-time haircut to any minister who was new to the area. Now, the people of Aardvark County were predominantly of the Baptist faith, even though there was a smattering of other faiths and religions. In the area around Groveville, in addition to the Baptist churches, there were congregations of Methodists Presbyterians, Catholics, Mormons, Jehovah's Witnesses, Church of Christ, Church of God, Church of God of Prophesy, Assembly of God, and the snake-handling church up in the edge of the mountains.

One day, the new priest from Our Savior Catholic Church came to Shorty's to get a haircut. When Shorty was finished, the priest asked him, "How much do I owe you?"

Shorty replied, "Nothing, Father, just say a prayer for me at your next mass." The next morning, when Shorty opened up his front door, there was a big fruit basket on the stoop with a note of thanks from the priest.

About a week later, the new pastor from Step of Faith Presbyterian Church came in to get a haircut. When Shorty finished the haircut, the pastor asked, "How much do I owe you?"

Once again, Shorty answered, "Nothing, Reverend. Just say a prayer for me when you go to church on Sunday." The next morning when Shorty opened his door, he found a big bunch of cut flowers from the pastor, thanking him for giving him a free haircut and making him feel welcome in the community.

About a month later, the First Baptist Church called a new pastor to minister to the people of Groveville. A couple of weeks later, he came to the barbershop, introduced himself, and told Shorty he needed a haircut. "How much do I owe you?" the pastor asked the barber when he had finished.

Shorty responded, "Nothing, Preacher. Just pray for me in church on Sunday." The next morning when he opened his door, he found on his stoop a big bunch of five Baptist preachers.

Gems of Wisdom
from The Old-Timer

There are two types of people in the world: Those who can sing and those who can't. May God have mercy on those who can't tell the difference.

Lying at the Barbershop

Shorty's Barber Shop in Groveville was – on Saturdays – the meeting place for loafers who had nothing else to do to pass the time of day. It was also the meeting place for some of the biggest liars in Aardvark County. Shorty Green (actually his real name was Clarence) hovered his six feet, four-inch frame over each of his customers to make sure that they received the proper grooming. Life was kind of laid back in Groveville. Because of busy work schedules, many of the men chose Saturdays to get their haircuts. No one was in a big hurry. If you wanted a haircut in a hurry, then you came on a Wednesday or Thursday. If you came to get a haircut on Saturday, and there were five customers ahead of you, that was perfectly all right because it gave you an opportunity to socialize. You had the privilege of seeing the hair cut short and the tales grow tall. Except for church and the lodge hall, there was no other place where the men could gather, without their wives, and have good clean fun.

One particular spring Saturday, some of us local regulars were gathered together at Shorty's. Some of the men were there to actually get a haircut. A few were there just to get their weekly dose of truth stretching. Among those present on that day were John Loutin, Colin Brown,

85

Ed Jenkins, and Jim "Moses" Barkley. Jim had been nicknamed "Moses" by a childhood friend who told him, "Every time you open your mouth, the bull rushes forth." Jim was a state game warden. He was also the king of storytelling. When he was holding court in the barber shop with one of his tales, he had everyone's undivided attention.

Colin Brown began spinning a yarn as Shorty cut his hair. It involved a man that he caught squirrel hunting on his property. The story went like this: "I was walking in the woods last fall over on the other side of my corn field. I came upon a man standing over near a big oak tree. Even though he was trespassing, I hid behind some bushes so I could see what he was up to. He didn't have a gun, so I didn't think he was actually hunting. He did have a gunny sack with him, so naturally, I was curious. As I watched, I saw a big gray squirrel run down out of that oak tree and run across the ground. When it got near the man, it keeled over at the man's feet – dead. He then picked up the squirrel and put it in the sack. I was very curious, but I didn't say anything. A little later, I saw another squirrel run down out of that tree and die right there at the man's feet. He picked up this squirrel and also put it in the bag. Still, I remained silent and hid in the bushes. About fifteen minutes later, I saw another squirrel run down out of that tree and fall dead at the stranger's feet. This time, I could keep quiet no longer. I came busting out of the bushes and confronted him. I said, 'Look here, Mister; I have seen three squirrels run down out of that oak tree and fall over dead at your feet. What in the world are you doing to kill them?'

The man replied, 'I just look at them and ugly them to death.'

I then told him, 'Yeah, I can understand that. You are probably the ugliest man I have ever seen in my life.'

The man went on, 'Yes sir, I used to bring my wife with me squirrel hunting, but she was so ugly that it got to where she tore the meat up too bad.'

Everyone got a good laugh out of that story. Colin paid Shorty for the haircut, but he didn't dare leave because he knew that Moses was next. Jim settled into the barber chair and for a while, folks thought that on this day, they would walk away disappointed. Jim did not begin a story right away. Then all at once, his faced lit up, and he began to spin a tale:

"Last summer, I was over at Simmons Lake checking fishing licenses. I came upon an older man fishing off the bank, near the boat ramp. I checked his license, and everything was in order. He had caught a couple of bass and bream, all within the limit. As I talked with him, he hooked a fish that I knew immediately was going to give him a fight. He played the fish a little until he thought it was tired out. He then tried to reel it in, but it was a struggle. After about fifteen minutes, the man still hadn't got the fish to the bank. All of a sudden, the fish jumped into the air, and I saw the biggest largemouth bass that I have ever seen in my life. I thought for a minute, the fish was going to drag the old codger in the lake, but he stood his ground. When the fish was about ten feet from the bank, I knew that if I didn't help the man, he was going to lose this fish. My truck had a winch on the front, and so I hurried over, released the cable, and drug it out in the water. I hooked the cable hook in the fish's gills. Then, I went back to the truck to turn the winch on. The cable tightened up, but still, the fish put up a fight. The winch was beginning to smoke, so I put the truck in reverse and backed up. Slowly, but surely, I drug the fish out of the water and up onto the bank.

When I went over to unhook the cable, the old man said to me, 'Mister Game Warden, I appreciate you helping me catch my fish, but to be honest with you, sir, I really ain't got no way to haul it home. Besides that, there ain't nobody there anymore but my wife and me, so we could never eat up all that much fish. Would you mind taking it for yourself?'

Well, I agreed to take the fish home with me. I turned the truck around and pulled the winch cable over the cab and hooked the fish once more. The fish was already tuckered out by this time, so it was easier to pull him up in the truck. I tied him down and started off. I hadn't gone more than a hundred yards when I realized that the fish's squirming was making the truck swerve. I pulled over, got my Smith & Wesson .22 out of my holster and shot that fish right in the head. When I got home, I climbed up in the truck so I could clean the fish in there. That's when I realized just how big this fish really was! I knew that my family would not be able to eat all of this fish either. I decided to give it to the Aardvark County Soup Kitchen. Of course, I kept the scales because I used them for shingles on the roof of my boathouse. The next week, the soup kitchen ran a notice in the newspaper, stating that they would not be able to accept food donations for an entire month until they got that fish used up."

Jim finished his story just as the barber finished his haircut. No one spoke a word. They all knew that they had just had a crash course in Advanced Lying 101. Jim paid Shorty for the haircut, got his hat from the hook, and started to leave. At the door, he turned and said, "Boys, remember; if you tell a lie, make it a big one."

"It was the biggest fish I had ever seen."

The Thief and the Liar

Jack Bailey was one of those rare individuals who would literally give you the shirt right off of his back. Everyone in Aardvark County knew him. He lived just outside the city limits of Groveville, where he had worked for many years as a mailman. Everyone in Groveville knew him, and often, they were the recipient of a kind word or a brief conversation, as he made his rounds. In the summer, ladies would often present him with a cold glass of tea as he delivered the mail. Little children sometimes picked dandelions and gave him their bouquets.

Even though Jack was a "salt of the earth" kind of guy, there was one thing that infuriated him. That was the idea that someone would steal from him. He was a hardworking man who had accumulated some things to make his life more comfortable. He was not rich by any means, but he was always willing to give to charities and to his church. If anyone needed to borrow something from him, all they had to do was ask. That is why he went into a rage when someone stole from him.

One Saturday, after Jack had finished his mail route, he decided to cut his grass. As he tried to crank his riding lawn mower, he discovered the battery was producing no power whatsoever. As he raised the mower's seat to investigate it, he made a startling discovery: there was no battery. The cables had been cut, and the battery was gone. Jack looked around and discovered that he was also missing a few tools and some jumper cables from his garage. He promptly called the police to report the theft.

By the time the police chief arrived, Jack was livid. He tried to imagine who would steal from him. It was obvious that the thief had taken things that could be sold quickly for cash. He thought of a house that he passed on his route every day. It was rumored that the people who lived there ran a pharmaceutical business. However, the pharmaceuticals were sold in little bags – not in bottles like at the drug store. Could some of these people's customers have been the thieves? Jack didn't know.

As the police chief filled out the loss report, Jack was still in a furor. He handed Jack a copy of the report and told him that he would be looking out for the stolen items. Jack told the policeman, "I hate to be stolen from, and if I catch someone stealing from me, I will fill his backside with birdshot from my twelve-gauge shotgun."

The policeman told him, "Okay, Jack, you do have the right to protect your property, but please, be careful."

That night Jack did not sleep much. His security had been violated. He wondered if someone had been watching his house. He also wondered if the thief would strike again. He finally fell into a fitful sleep an hour before dawn.

Jack awoke that Sunday morning with a nagging feeling that he had said something wrong to the policeman. Being a religious man, he felt convicted in his heart that he had sinned. He went to church that day and after the service, asked to speak with Pastor Laster. As he sat in the pastor's study, Jack related the details of the robbery. He also told the preacher about his statement to the police chief concerning the twelve-gauge shotgun. He also stated that he felt ugly inside because he felt that he had sinned. The kind pastor talked with Jack and assured him that his feelings were normal for someone such as he who had been so violated. He then told Jack that God would forgive him of any sin that was confessed to Him. He prayed with Jack, asking God to help him with his attitude and to help him have a forgiving spirit. He then asked God to forgive Jack for having bad thoughts against his fellow man.

When Pastor Laster finished praying, Jack sat there with a puzzled look on his face. "Is there anything else I can help you with, Jack?" the pastor asked.

"Yes, Pastor, there is," replied Jack. "I don't think you fully understand the situation here. I still intend to shoot anybody that I catch stealing from me. The thing that convicted me was the sin of lying. You see, I don't own a twelve-gauge shotgun. My gun is a sixteen-gauge."

Special Message From The Old-Timer

To the thief who stole my gas can from my garage: I wish to inform you that now I have purchased two identical gas cans. One of them is filled with gas. The other one is filled with water and sugar. Which one is which? Only I know! Do you feel lucky, Punk? Go ahead, make my day!

The Young Preacher

Calvin Belcher was a young man who went to the First Community Fellowship Church where the Rev. A. T. Laster was the pastor. Calvin came from a backwoods sort of family who did not put much emphasis on education. There had never been a single high school graduate in his family. His family was involved in the logging industry, so Calvin had grown up working hard with his father cutting pulpwood. Calvin had gone to school, but often was absent because his father needed him to help out with the business. As a result of this, Calvin formally dropped out of school in the eighth grade at age sixteen to work with his father cutting wood. He had failed several grades, and his folks thought it was a waste of time and money for him to continue his education. The really sad thing about Calvin was the fact that he was actually a functional illiterate, reading only on the second grade level.

Now, Calvin's father, although not keen on book learning, insisted that his children go to church and learn about God. He considered himself a God-fearing man, even though he did not attend church on a regular basis. Pastor Laster had bought an old school bus and had it painted purple. He had a sign painted on the side which read: The Big Purple People Picker-Upper. He used this bus to pick up people for church services. This was often Calvin's ride to church. Something really good came out of Pastor Laster's bus ministry. When Calvin was seventeen years old, he felt God was calling him to be a preacher. He arranged to have a talk with Pastor Laster to discuss what was on his mind.

When Calvin met with the preacher, Pastor Laster offered both encouragement and advice. He told Calvin that if he was certain that he was being called into the ministry, God would surely provide for him and use him. He advised him that it would be a difficult task because he would need to do a lot of studying and reading. He then assured Calvin that he was willing to help him any way he could. Pastor Laster was really concerned about how much Calvin knew about the Bible, so he point blank asked him, "Calvin, do you know the Bible well?"

"Yes, Pastor," Calvin replied. "I know the Bible from cover to cover."

"What is your favorite part?" asked the pastor.

Calvin then told him, "I like the parables best, sir."

Pastor Laster asked, "Calvin, what is your favorite parable?"

Calvin answered, "My favorite parable is The Parable of the Good Samaritan."

Pastor Laster then asked Calvin, "Can you tell me the story of the Good Samaritan?"

Calvin said, "Yes, I can. It seems that this man went down to Jericho, and he fell among thorns. The thorns sprang up and choked him and left him for dead. A priest and a Levite came along and dragged him out of the city. Then, a Samaritan came along and gave him some wine and put him on his donkey. Then, he rode him along until they got on good ground. The man tried to pay the Samaritan, but he refused any money. All he said was, 'Go thou and do likewise.' After the Samaritan left, he went to Nineveh and preached about the blessings of the Lord. The people of Nineveh received the blessings of the Lord— some twentyfold, some fiftyfold, and some a hundredfold.

"After he left Nineveh, he went on three or four missionary journeys before he died. On one of these journeys, he saw old Queen Jezebel sitting high and lifted up in a window. So he screamed, 'Y'all throw her down out of there.' So, they threw her down. Then, he said, 'Throw her down again.' They threw her down seventy times seven times. And because she fell on stony ground, they picked up twelve baskets of the fragments that remained of her. Now, whose wife do you think she will be on Judgment Day?"

When Calvin finished his story, Pastor Laster sat speechless for a little while. Finally, he said, "Calvin, it's obvious that you have the Word of God in you, but son, we've got to get you some education so you'll be able to get it out straight."

Pastor Laster did what he said he would do and really helped Calvin. The first thing that he did was to make sure that Calvin went back to school. It was a hard struggle, but Pastor Laster finally convinced Calvin's folks that an education was important. He also arranged for Calvin to have a tutor so that he could learn to read better. It took a lot of hard work, but with the help of night school adult education, in three years Calvin, had a bona-fide high school diploma. During this time, Pastor Laster had taken Calvin under his wing to more fully teach him about the Bible. Pastor Laster also was instrumental in getting Calvin enrolled in a Bible college.

Finally, the day came when Calvin preached his first sermon. Pastor Laster arranged for him to preach at a Sunday night service at the church. He did fairly well for his first attempt at preaching, and the pastor was mighty proud of him. Calvin did make one major mistake at the end of his message that caused some of the folks to scratch their heads and say, "Huh?"

Calvin's idol had always been Billy Graham. He always imagined himself preaching to large crowds just like the Rev. Graham. In his excitement to invite people to make a decision for Christ, he imagined that he was speaking to a big crowd like the evangelist. In his invitation, he said, "Thousands of you are coming from all over this great arena. You are coming from the balconies; you are coming from all over. Do not be afraid to step out into the aisle. If you came here on a bus, the busses will wait." Now folks, the only problem with that statement was this: First of all, the church would only seat about three hundred people. Secondly, there was no balcony. The third and biggest problem was the fact that the only bus around was The Big Purple People Picker-Upper. The good news is that – after that first sermon – Calvin settled down and became a good preacher, and he was able to pastor a church for many years.

Calvin Belcher's First Sermon

*Why a Person Doesn't Need to Wait for the Hearse
to Carry Them to Church*

If you wait for the hearse to carry you to church:

- There will be flowers there, but you can't smell them.
- Your friends will be there, but you can't greet them.
- There will be beautiful music, but you can't enjoy it.
- The preacher will preach a sermon, but you won't be able to hear it.
- Your family will cry, but you can't comfort them.
- You will want another chance, but it will be too late.

A Good Name

Red Byrd was a man who had worked for many years for Dixie Textile Corporation. His real name was Fred Byrd, but because of his auburn hair and freckles, when he was young, he was nicknamed "Red." In fact, he had endured a lot of nicknames throughout the years including "Fred the Red," "Fred the Redneck," and even "Byrdbrain." Most folks just called him "Red," and he seemed content with that.

It was ironic that Red's last name was Byrd, because birds were his hobby. When he was in school, he would scribble drawings of birds when he was bored with his studies. He was fascinated by birds of all kinds, not just exotic ones like parrots and parakeets. He really enjoyed being outdoors so he could observe the birds in their natural habitats. He helped them out by buying birdseed and building houses and feeders for them.

When Red finished high school and entered the workforce, he continued to observe and care for his feathered friends. He continued, through the years, building birdhouses which he used, sold, or gave away. His garden was a regular haven for the birds because he planted sunflowers and other nice things that the birds loved. He was often seen at the flea markets across the county, selling his birdhouses and feeders, as well as bags of his homegrown sunflower seeds. Red was also largely responsible for having the Aardvark County Garden Club declare Groveville an official bird sanctuary.

When Red had been at his textile job about twenty years, the company went into an economic decline. Red's job was downsized, and he was laid off. Although the company promised to rehire the workers when business picked up, Red realized that the textile industry was on shaky ground. There was no security in textiles, as several mills across the state had already closed their doors.

As Red experienced his first weeks of unemployment, he began to think about his future. He had heard somewhere that if a person found something that he was passionate about, and he did that for a living, he would be happy for the rest of his life. Red realized that his passion was birds. After much soul-searching, Red decided to go out on a limb and invest his nest-egg savings in a bird supply business.

Red found a suitable shop that was for sale in Groveville. With the help of his savings and a bank loan, he purchased the building and went about starting his bird business. He was able to line up suppliers for birdseed and fancy bird houses. He also stocked birdbaths, books on birds and their care, and just about anything else you could think of in the bird supply line. Of course, he continued to sell his homemade birdhouses and sunflower seeds. His shop also carried a line of framed bird prints and wooden carvings, many of which he had carved himself. In the spring, he added vegetable plants and other garden supplies to his inventory. These were really good sellers on sunny days when the folks of Aardvark County developed "farming fever," after having been inside all winter.

Amazingly, Red's business was profitable from the start. In about two years, he was able to pay off his loan and own the building free and clear. What was truly amazing was the fact that a specialty shop like Red's could prosper in a little insignificant town like Groveville. What was the secret of Red's success? After a few years in business, when people began to analyze Red's shop and ask why it was so successful, they could not come up with a clear answer. Was it the location? They agreed that this probably was not the reason. After all, this was Aardvark County, not exactly the tourist center of the world. Could it be Red's personality? This was a possible answer, but folks agreed that Red did not have a dynamic personality. In fact, he appeared to be a little eccentric to some people. When all was said and done, the general consensus was that there were two main factors that contributed to Red's business success. The first one was that he worked hard and enthusiastically for something that he was passionate about. The second contributing factor was the name that Red chose for his business. He had thought long and hard about what to call his shop. He had rejected the names of "Byrd's Nest," "Byrd's House," and even "The Robin Hood." In a sudden flash of insight, Red had come up with the perfect name – one that would be recognized all over America. He named his place "Wren Dixie."

Gems of Wisdom
from The Old-Timer

Birds have bills too, but they keep on singing.

Getting Married and Buried

The Celestial Valley Funeral Home and Wedding Chapel, located in Aardvark County, was owned and operated by Stanley Anderson and his brother Walden. Stanley was the young man who had blown up the church's outhouse while on furlough from the Army during WWII. After his release from the Army, he had gone off to school and became a licensed funeral director and embalmer. His younger brother had followed in his footsteps and had also gone into the funeral business. For many years, they worked for someone else at the funeral home. Then due to the owner's retirement, the brothers were able to buy the business for themselves.

Now, Walden was also an ordained minister. There had been many a time when he would conduct a funeral for someone as the preacher and then, assist in the funeral director's capacity with the burial. Shortly after the brothers took possession of the business, they realized that there were often idle times when no one in the community had died. As morbid as it sounded, they were at the mercy of the public to stay in business. Stanley had even been known to joke, "I don't wish anybody any bad luck, but I sure hope business picks up."

It was about this time that the brothers hit on an idea.

They decided to rent out their funeral chapel as a wedding chapel. It became the setting for couples who wanted a small, quiet wedding, without the fancy fanfare. Walden performed some of these ceremonies himself, often with just the groom and bride in attendance. The couple also had the privilege of securing their own minister or notary public to officiate.

Every preacher probably has a collection of stories about funny things that have happened at weddings or funerals. The Anderson brothers were doubly blessed in their collection of stories because they had the benefit of having two businesses, which gave them an abundance of comic material.

One of the most memorable weddings that Walden participated in was the time he married what he called the "farm couple." These folks had made arrangements for their simple ceremony about a week in advance. When this couple came for their wedding, they were dressed in regular farm clothes. He wore blue overalls and a red plaid shirt. The bride had on a print dress with no extra frills or elaborations. To their credit, both the overalls and the dress appeared to be new. They seemed to act like this was no special occasion. It just appeared that this was another thing on their long list of things that they had to do that day – slop the hogs, feed the chickens, go get married, and milk the cows.

After the ceremony, the groom asked Walden, "Preacher, how much do I owe you?"

Walden replied, "I always tell the groom that he can pay whatever he thinks his new wife is worth."

The man then reached in his pocket and pulled out a dollar bill, which he gave to the preacher. He said, "Here, Preacher, take this dollar. I don't have any change." Walden looked at the happy bride for a moment. Then, he pulled some quarters from his own pocket and gave the man back fifty cents.

Funerals are sad events. There is nothing funny about a person dying. There are times, however, when things happen during the course of a funeral ceremony that, looking back, can be considered hilarious.

The Celestial Valley Funeral Home provided a standard obituary notice in the local paper for the deceased. The family also had the option of writing their own obituary notice for the deceased if they so desired. Sometimes, the obituary notices were very descriptive, telling how the deceased loved a particular sports team, Elvis, car racing, or even how they played checkers and horseshoes up until the day that they died.

A local citizen of Groveville named Jim Brown died. When the Andersons were telling the widow about all the options the funeral home offered, she decided to make up the wording of her late husband's obituary. The notice said: Jim Brown died on Monday; will be buried on Wednesday. When Stanley informed her that she could say a lot more if she so chose at no extra cost, she added some new information. The new notice read: Jim Brown died on Monday; will be buried on Wednesday. White Cadillac and Clemson-Florida State game tickets for sale.

One of the strangest funeral services that the Anderson brothers conducted was a graveside service with "makeshift military rites." Several men in Aardvark County enjoyed the sports of hunting and fishing. Among these was a man named Thomas "Tooth-nary" Thomas. He had been nicknamed Tooth-nary by his friends because he didn't have any teeth (as in nary a one). Thomas had no family, being a bachelor all his life. The people that he considered family were his close friends and hunting buddies. Thomas really loved to hunt and fish, so he would spend all his spare time in the woods or at the lake. He was a member of a hunt club and often went with his friends on deer drives in the fall. He also hunted squirrel and rabbit in the winter and turkeys in the spring. He had even been known to kill a couple of bears.

As he got older, Thomas developed some medical problems including diabetes and a heart condition. His condition worsened, and eventually, he had to go live in a nursing home. Thomas's one desire was that when he died, he would have a military rites funeral with the twenty-one gun salute. The only problem was that Thomas had never served in the military. You might say that the United States Government is being picky, but they have this little rule that says only people that are serving in the Armed Services – or have an honorable discharge – can have a military rites funeral. When Thomas died, his hunt club buddies wanted to honor their friend's request, so they got permission from Stanley Anderson to hold a special, country-style, Aardvark County twenty-one gun salute for their friend.

The only one in the group of his friends who had ever served in the military was Bubba Brunson. Bubba kind of took charge of the situation. He organized seven of Thomas's closest hunting friends to participate in the services. At the graveside, after the preacher had said a few nice words about Thomas, Bubba and the other seven men that he had rounded up marched across the ground toward the grave. These men had been drilled by Bubba until they could act just like a company of precision soldiers.

In real military life, the twenty-one gun salute is done with rifles. At Thomas's funeral, the weapon of choice was a twelve-gauge automatic shotgun. In real life, the guns are loaded with blanks. Nobody in Aardvark County had any blank shells. Why would anybody possess blank shells in Aardvark County? Either you hunted to kill or you didn't! In the absence of blank shells, Bubba's troop had loaded their guns with No. 8 field load shells, which are used to hunt squirrels and rabbits. So, across the ground, this fearless group marched over to the grave, just opposite a grove of big oak trees. At Bubba's command of "Company, halt," the men stopped. Then, at Bubba's command of "Company, aim," the men aimed their guns skyward toward the oak trees. Bubba then yelled, "Company, fire." In unison, the seven guns roared. Twice more, Bubba issued the command to fire, and twice more, the guns roared. The shooters felt a rush of joy and satisfaction that they had been able to honor their friend. All in all, it was a very fine service for Thomas "Tooth-nary" Thomas to be honored this way. There was something else that happened that day that also served to honor the hunter. Just as the last volley was heard from the shotguns, there was a rustling in the leaves of the oak trees, and three big squirrels fell dead from the tree and landed belly up on the ground — a very fitting end to a service for a great American sportsman such as Thomas.

The Street Corner Poet

There were living in Aardvark County several folks who had an unusual talent for being creative as far as the fine arts were concerned. The county folks were mighty proud of Andy Smith, who had painted the portrait of Custer's last stand for the bank president. They were equally proud of a young man named Robbie Woodruff. Robbie's claim to fame lay in the fact that he had the talent to write poetry. Ever since he was in grammar school, he had developed the ability to be able to put words together in a concise fashion. Even in normal conversations, he had a tendency to say things that rhymed. Of course, this sometimes annoyed people when he was growing up. Because many of his schoolmates got fed up with his corny rhymes, they nicknamed him "Hallmark." This nickname stuck with him the remainder of his life. His teachers were sometimes annoyed by his conversation as well. However, for the most part, they tried to encourage his creativity, realizing that the young man in their classes might well turn out to be the greatest literary genius of all time.

Robbie's parents were the proprietors of a family-run grocery store located at the corner of Crescent Avenue and South Main Street in Groveville. It was here that he learned the value of hard work, for he worked hard to help his parents in their business after school and on Saturdays. At the store, he was sometimes allowed to put his talent as a wordsmith to good use because his dad let him make up signs for the stores' specials. Folks would often chuckle at the humorous ads that Robbie came up with, and this made their shopping experience more enjoyable.

Not only did Robbie learn the value of hard work, but also the value of making money. He realized that he could take his talent as a poet and turned it into cold hard cash. That is why, at age thirteen, he persuaded his dad to give him a little corner of the store next to the office so he could set up a poem shop. Robbie set up a desk in the corner and promptly hung up a sign that read, Robbie Woodruff, The Street Corner Poet. Another sign advertised that he was willing to make up homemade poems and verses for those who had a hard time expressing their true feelings. Let's face facts: Aardvark County was not exactly the education center of the universe, so many people needed help in this area. Robbie worked out a deal with the owner of a print shop down the street so he could have an ample supply of his poems on the desk for sale.

There were many young men in Aardvark County who hired Robbie as their personal poet, so that they could have a sweet verse to give to their true love on Valentine's Day, or on any other special occasion. There was often repeat business, because as we all know, sometimes, true love does not last forever. Robbie had written four different love poems for one young man in a year, due mainly to the fickleness of "true love." Of course, this worked out to Robbie's advantage because he could always recycle a poem from a customer and have it printed to sell to someone else.

One particular person who availed himself of Robbie's services was a young man named Tommy Whiteford. Tommy and his girlfriend, Cissy, had been dating for three years. Tommy felt that it was time for their relationship to move to a whole new level. At a complete loss for words to express his true feelings for Cissy, he asked Robbie to come up with a special poem for his girlfriend. Robbie thought for a day on this one and came up with a poem that went like this:

Her Name

I carved my sweetie's name on a tree.
It was a special place for her and me.
But the tree withered and died one day,
And then it was cut down and hauled away.
Then to the high mountains I did go,
And wrote her name in the cold white snow.
But the snow melted as it often will,
So her name ran down the hill.
Then I went to where the ocean meets the land,
And drew her name there in the sand.
Though it was written as pretty as could be,
My sweetie's name went out to sea.
Then I cried to my God above,
"Where can I write the name of my true love?"
Then a voice came so clear it gave me a start,
"Her name is already written on your heart."
So now I realize her name is a part of me,
Forever, always, and eternally.

When Tommy gave Cissy the poem, he also gave her another gift. When she read the poem and had stopped crying, Tommy got down on one knee, presented her with the other gift – a diamond engagement ring–and asked her to marry him. Then, she said "yes" and cried some more. Tommy was so overjoyed that the next day he came into the store and gave Robbie a twenty-dollar tip.

Another person who realized the potential in Tommy's talent for the usage of words was Pastor Laster. He arranged for Tommy to be in charge of coming up with sayings for the message board on the church sign that they had recently purchased. Some of Tommy's sign board messages were blunt and to the point, but they seemed to have an impact on a lot of lives in Aardvark County. Some of the best of them were these:

- God allows EWE turns for all His sheep
- Before they bury you in the hole, make sure Jesus has your soul.
- Before they lay you beneath the sod, you better give your life to God.
- May the Lord bless and keep you until the undertaker comes to get you.
- Give your heart to Jesus today, or there will be hell to pay.
- About life's treasures don't be boasting, or in hell, you'll be roasting.

And so, folks, that is how the Street Corner Poet of Aardvark County came to be. Robbie Woodruff, the grocery store boy, made it big in the world through his ability to put together words in a pleasing manner. Robbie eventually went to college and later, he actually went to work for Hallmark. After doing that for a while, he became an English professor at a college in upstate New York. It was here that he continued to write poems and became famous as a published author of poetry books. There was only one time, as far as Robbie could remember, that the writing of a poem worked out to his disadvantage. It happened when Robbie was a freshman in college. He fell madly in love with a beautiful co-ed in his English class. They dated for a few weeks, and then Robbie wrote her a Valentine's Day poem. It went like this:

To my Valentine

As Valentine's Day approached, I found myself in a
terrible pickle,
Until I bought this card for two quarters and a nickel.
I picked for you a lovely flower,
But it was dead within the hour.
The flower's scent will soon be gone,
Bur your smell will go on and on.
I would swim the ocean wide,
Just to catch a glimpse of your lovely hide.
I would wade the deepest river;
I'd suffer through heart disease, pneumonia, or cirrhosis
of the liver.
I'd go through agony and I'd go through pain;
I will see you on Saturday if it doesn't rain.

Robbie's girlfriend broke up with him, but she didn't tell him why. Perhaps, for Valentine's Day, instead of a poem, she wanted a rose, but, hey, that's how it goes!

The Prison Ministry

Gus Oscarweitzer was a good friend of Pastor Laster. He was a member of the First Community Fellowship Church in Groveville. Gus was also a chaplain at the Riverside Correctional Institute, one of the state's prison facilities in Aardvark County. Because he had such a long last name, he was referred to as "Rev. Gus," or "Chaplain O."

One day, Pastor Laster was talking with Gus about the possibility of starting a church ministry at the prison. Gus agreed that it would be a good thing to do and arranged for the pastor to take a tour of the prison. Now, Gus had an unusual sense of humor, and was not above playing a joke on those that he was close to. Prior to Pastor Laster's visit, Gus secured the help of a few of the inmates to help pull a prank on him.

When Pastor Laster arrived at the prison, Gus gave him the grand tour. As they went out into a courtyard, the pastor saw a group of inmates standing around in a group and laughing. Unknown to him, these men were part of the chaplain's prank. Someone in the group would yell out a number, and the rest of the men would laugh. Then someone else would yell out a number, and they would laugh again.

"What are they doing, Gus?" the pastor asked.

"Well," said Gus, "in here, the men don't get much opportunity to hear new jokes, so they have all their old jokes numbered. To save time, someone just calls out a number; the rest of the men remember the joke, and everyone laughs. Say, Pastor, I have an idea. Why don't you go over and tell one? Try number fifty-seven. That's a good one."

So Pastor Laster walked over to the group and shouted, "Number fifty-seven!" Instead of laughter, no one spoke a word. The men gave the preacher some menacing looks. He ran back to Gus and said, "Gus, what did I do? Those men look like they are going to kill me!"

With a grin, Gus said, "Well, you know how it is. Some preachers just can't tell a joke."

After that first day, Pastor Laster began a successful prison ministry. He visited the inmates on a regular basis, and once a month, volunteers from the church led in Sunday afternoon worship services.

There was at notable prisoner at Riverside by the name of Frank Hickson. Frank was a lifer. He had been found guilty of first-degree murder and had received a sentence of life without parole. Frank had never tried to blame anyone else for his situation. He was not one of those people who blamed his parents, his economic conditions, or his social status for the fact that he was in lock-up. He only blamed himself, his stupidity, and his short-fused temper for his predicament.

After the prison ministry started, Frank began to notice that some of the inmates, who were regular Sunday afternoon worship service attendees, seemed to be happier and easier to get along with. They seemed as if they had a good time at the services. Frank had never been very keen on church going, but he always enjoyed having a good time. He had heard that one of his fellow inmates had "got religion," so he sought him out to talk about the experience. His friend told him about how his entire attitude had changed and how he now had love in his heart for his fellow man. Then, Frank asked him, "How does a person get to be like this?"

His friend was new in the faith and didn't know a whole lot about the Bible, so he told Frank, "All I know is that if a person really wants to live for God, the first thing he has to do is talk to Pastor Laster."

The next time the church had a prison worship service, Frank went to the chapel to check out the situation. He heard the singing and listened to Pastor Laster's sermon. When the service was over, he went back to his cell and thought about what he had heard. It was all very interesting, but he didn't think it was for him. After all, he was a lifer.

The following week, the pastor was visiting the prison and met Frank. They talked for a while, but Frank informed the preacher that he had no intention of changing his ways. However, at the next service, Frank was once again there. After the service, Frank asked the preacher, "Why are you always trying to chip away at me? I know you preached that sermon just to make me feel bad." Pastor Laster assured Frank that he was not picking on him, but merely trying to preach the gospel.

When the pastor visited the prison again, Frank

thought of a good question for him. He asked, kind of smart-alecky, "Tell me something here, Preacher. When I was a baby, my mother had me baptized in the Presbyterian Church. If I was to accept your religion, would that baptism work for me? You'd probably want to dunk me in the pool again, wouldn't you?"

Pastor Laster told Frank, "Before we discuss baptism, we need to talk about being born again."

And then, Frank asked the simple question, "So what does a person do to be born again?"

A smile came across the face of Pastor Laster, and right there, he explained to Frank how a person becomes born again. And so, kneeling there with Pastor Laster, with only the cell bars separating them, Frank asked Jesus into his heart and received his spiritual freedom.

Immediately, the prison officials and inmates noticed a change in Frank. One day, another friend saw Frank and asked him, "Frank what has come over you?"

Frank replied, "I've got life."

The friend responded, "But Frank, the judge gave you life ten years ago."

"I know that," said Frank, "But now life has got me."

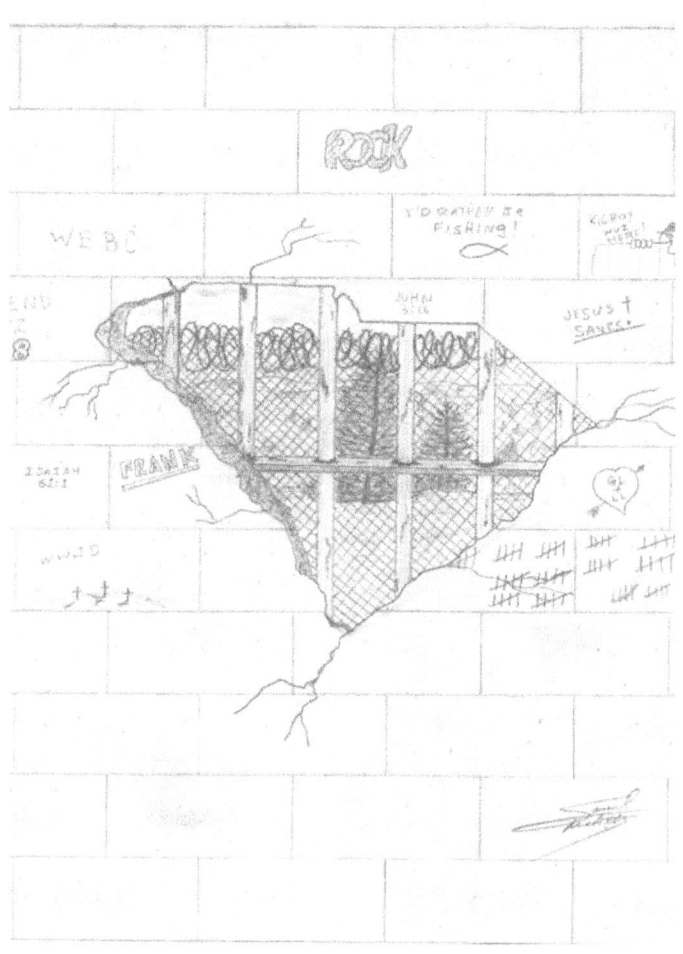

Graffiti on the wall of Riverside Correctional Institute
(after Frank got "life")

The Possum in the Pew

The First Community Fellowship Church always welcomed visitors. One Sunday, however, there was a visitor that was most unwelcome. Mrs. Rosa Domingo Jones attended the church faithfully and always sat in the fourth pew from the front on the right side. Rosa was fluent in three languages. Her father was from Venezuela and spoke Spanish. Her mother was from Rome, Italy, and spoke Italian as her mother tongue. Her parents had moved to America to live in the land of opportunity shortly before Rosa's birth. The end result was that Rosa grew up in a household where she heard Italian, Spanish, and English on a regular basis. Her desire to be a teacher had led her to an opening in Aardvark County where she taught Spanish at the high school. It was here that she met and married Arnold Jones, who also was a teacher.

On this particular Sunday, Rosa came to church as usual. She often missed Sunday School, but was faithful to attend the morning worship service. She arrived at the church about fifteen minutes early and mingled with the other worshippers as they made their way to their seats. Rosa sat in her usual spot and did not pay attention to anything unusual in the pew. She set her purse on the pew and turned to talk to a friend. While she was still talking, she reached for her purse to retrieve a tissue, but she touched something fuzzy instead. She looked down and saw a huge possum just waking up from a long winter's nap. (Here, in Aardvark County, we still spell possum with a "p," just like Adam did when God told him to name all the animals in the Garden of Eden.)

Throughout the church, everyone heard a high-pitched scream. Folks came running from everywhere to see what had happened. At the first sound of the scream, the possum jumped down and ran under the pew. Rosa jumped and landed on the pew. For a few minutes, pandemonium reigned. There were those that day that originally thought Rosa was speaking in a heavenly language. Then, they realized the words that were coming from Rosa's mouth were not spiritual. The gospel truth is that poor Rosa forgot that she was in the house of the Lord.

Rosa began to cuss in three languages. First came the Italian and then, the Spanish. By the time Rosa got around to the English language, the people could understand her a lot better. By this time, there were other people standing on the pews. Rosa's cussing spree ran the gamut from talking about the possum's maternal heritage to describing body parts and functions. Her language was so bad, it would have made a restroom graffiti artist blush. Most of the congregation had heard all of those words before, but they had never heard them strung together like Rosa did it.

About that time, Mr. John Loutin entered the sanctuary with his faithful dog Buster. Buster immediately took in the situation and made a dive for the possum. The possum started running laps around the sanctuary with the dog in hot pursuit. Folks were still jumping on the pews to get out of the melee. Finally, someone opened the door, and the possum and the dog ran outside. Buster took a flying leap from the church porch and attacked the critter before it could run away. The animals rolled over and over on the ground. Finally, though scratched and cut, Buster emerged victorious. The possum lay dead on the ground.

After the commotion, Rosa left the church and went home. She was embarrassed by what she had said in the excitement of the moment. Mr. John Loutin also left to take Buster to Dr. Abercrombie to get stitched up. Pastor Laster did not preach his prepared sermon that morning. Everyone was so shook up, he tried to offer some words of comfort. He also encouraged the people to be understanding and forgiving toward Rosa. He told the congregation that any one of them might have acted the same way if they had been in Rosa's shoes.

After Rosa got home, she determined in her heart that she was never going to that church again. She felt that she had made a fool of herself in front of everybody. She was so embarrassed that she did not see how she could ever show her face there again.

An amazing thing happened to Rosa that week, though. She received ten visits from people of the congregation encouraging her not to quit church. She also received twenty-one phone calls from her friends showing their love and encouragement.

The next Sunday, Rosa was back in church. However, she looked at the pew cautiously before she sat down. As

Pastor Laster began the service, he announced, "Ladies and gentlemen, we have a hero in our midst today. We also have someone who wants to give him a special presentation. The hero is Buster. Mr. John, bring Buster to the front, please." Mr. John led Buster to the front of the church. Then, Rosa came forward and placed a medallion on a red ribbon around Buster's neck. The inscription on the medallion read: To Buster, the Defender of the Faithful. Rosa then gave Buster a big hug. Everyone rose to their feet and applauded. Rosa just said, "Hallelujah," which is the same word in all languages.

Gems of Wisdom
from The Old-Timer

Gumption is that thing in a coon dog that keeps him from barking up a tree when there ain't no coon up there.

Getting a Kick Out of Life

One of the odd things about Colin Brown, a farmer in Aardvark County, was the fact that he had walked with a limp for almost forty years. When he was sixteen years old, he had an accident on his daddy's farm that left him with a bent left leg. His daddy plowed with a mule, so as Colin grew older, he also learned how to use the mules to help with the farm work. As he got into his teen years, he was doing his share of the plowing and other farm work.

One of the favorite pastimes, for folks in Aardvark County in those days, was to go to the movies on Saturday afternoon. Mr. Brown believed in hard work, but once a month, he allowed his children to have a Saturday afternoon off – if their chores were done – to go to the movies. This was also the time that he and Mrs. Brown went to town to buy groceries and supplies. Colin especially liked the cowboy movies. He enjoyed seeing The Lone Ranger and Roy Rogers, but his favorite cowboy of all time was Gene Autry. On occasion, when he would bring the mules in from the fields, he would ride them and pretend that he was Gene Autry, riding tall in the saddle.

One day, when he had finished plowing for the day, Colin unhooked the plow and singletree from the mule and left them at the edge of the field. He had been plowing with Old Beck, his daddy's aging mule, who was almost blind. Now, Old Beck had never taken kindly to anyone riding him, but Colin rode him anyway. After all, in his mind's eye, he was Gene Autry, the bigger-than-life, bullet-proof, king of the cowboys, riding tall in the saddle.

When he rode into the barnyard, he saw his sister feeding the chickens. He hollered out to her and said, "Look here, Sis. This is how Gene Autry gets off his horse." Having said that, he proceeded to dismount the mule by sliding backwards over its backside. He had just cleared the mule's hindquarters when Old Beck decided that this was not appropriate behavior. The mule came across with a back kick that sent Colin sailing through the air.

At first, Colin was knocked senseless. For a while, he was conscious only of the fact that he was going upward toward the barn roof. Everything seemed to be playing out in slow motion. He cleared the mulberry bush that was growing by the barn. As he continued on his flight, he imagined that he saw the mice in the barn loft holding their breath. In their little mouse-like hearts, they knew that this was not going to turn out good. Colin actually thought that he was dead and that he was going to heaven. As he cleared the barn loft, something happened that stopped his heavenly ascent. That "something" is called the law of gravity. Colin began to fall toward the ground, faster, he believed, than when he went up. As he plummeted down, he was fully conscious just before he hit, but then lost consciousness again at the time of impact.

When Colin came to, the doctor was there, and he was lying in his own bed. His leg was broken in three places, but other than that, he was going to be okay. As he recuperated in bed for the next few days, he did a lot of thinking about two things. The first thing was why being knocked senseless hurt so much. The second thing was how he could have ever thought that a two-bit, no-good cowboy like Gene Autry could be his hero.

The story had a happy ending. Because of Colin's broken leg, he was excused from plowing the rest of the summer. More good news was that the Brown family had fried chicken three times that week, (and it wasn't even Sunday) due to the heroic efforts of three Rhode Island Reds who courageously gave their lives to break Colin's fall.

The Missing Leaf

Pastor Laster was well respected in the community. His congregation dearly loved him because of his tremendous abilities in pastoral care. There were many families around Groveville who had experienced his compassion and love in times of need. The First Community Fellowship Church had grown through the years, due partly to the ministry of this hardworking pastor.

Though he was an excellent pastor, Pastor Laster was not a powerful preacher. He knew the Bible well, but even after many years, he still experienced nervousness in the pulpit. He had been known to get his words mixed up, and at times, had lost his train of thought. For this reason, he had developed the habit of writing out his sermons and notes. This kept him focused, so that he was able, most of the time, to say exactly what he wanted to say.

One day, after his sermon, when he was greeting the people at the door, a little girl told him, "Pastor Laster, when I grow up and get a job, I'm going to give you lots of money."

Puzzled, the pastor asked the little girl, "Honey, why would you want to give me money?"

The child replied, "Because my daddy said that you were the poorest preacher he has ever heard."

When Pastor Laster wrote the manuscripts for his sermons, he put them in a loose-leaf notebook. He found that this was the most convenient way for him, because the pages were easy to turn. It was a little known fact that on Saturday afternoons, the pastor would go to the church and read his sermon aloud to see how it sounded. This way, he actually "practiced what he preached." The preacher had also developed the habit of leaving his precious notebook on the pulpit, ready for Sunday morning. He did not want to run the risk of leaving his sermon at home, for without his notes, he was lost.

One of the ones who knew about Pastor Laster's Saturday afternoon secret was Luanne Chester, the church custodian. She had, on occasion, caught the pastor practicing his sermon, when she came to clean the church for the Sunday service. Luanne, a single parent, often brought her teenage son Jonathan with her to help her clean the church. Jonathan had been known to get into trouble from time to time, so Luanne brought him along to keep an eye on him.

One Saturday, the pastor was just finishing rehearsing his sermon when Luanne and Jonathan arrived at the church. He closed his notebook, bid them a good afternoon, and left. On this day, Jonathan was supposed to be dusting the pews while his mother cleaned the Sunday school rooms. He kept noticing the notebook on the pulpit and wondered what was inside. An idea suddenly came to him that, surely, came from Satan himself. For no other reason, other than it seemed funny at the time, Jonathan tore a page out of the notebook and threw it in the trash.

The next morning, the services proceeded as usual.

"Hey! One of my leaves is missing!"

The Sunday school teachers taught their hearts out to sleepy classes, some men grabbed a quick smoke after the class, and everyone convened in the sanctuary for the worship service. The choir did an excellent job, and everyone settled back for the sermon.

Sometimes preachers seem to have an inkling that some sermons will be better than others. Pastor Laster was pleased with himself, because he felt that this was one of his best sermons ever. The message was from the book of Genesis, where God expelled Adam and Eve from the Garden of Eden. At this point, he did not know that an important page had been pilfered from the pulpit. As he read along, the congregation heard these words, "And Adam said to Eve, his wife . . . " Pastor Laster turned the page and continued, "Hey, one of my leaves is missing."

Instantly, small beads of panic perspiration broke out on Pastor Laster's brow. A few folks chuckled, not sure if this was a joke or not. After what seemed like an eternity, he regained his composure and said, "Well, I'll know not to use that joke again." He then proceeded boldly into the next page as if nothing had happened. He was mighty relieved when the sermon was over, and when he pronounced the benediction, he silently gave thanks for the special help from above.

The people never really understood what happened to the pastor's message that day. Some folks just chalked it up to another example of his train of thought being derailed. Pastor Laster never could prove who had altered his message, but he had his suspicions. From that day forward, however, he kept his notebook under lock and key until the appropriate time.

Lucky Eddie

Eddie Wilson was one of those people who never managed to get ahead in life, financially. He seemed to be forever behind on the payment of his bills, even though he worked hard every day. There never seemed to be enough money to go around. He inwardly was often envious of other folks in Aardvark County who had nicer houses and drove nicer cars. He had sarcastically nicknamed himself "Lucky Eddie," after the character in the comic strip "Hagar the Horrible" because he felt that he was doomed to be a member of the poor class forever. Eddie had tried second jobs in multi-level marketing business deals, but they had never worked out to his advantage. His philosophy in life was this: Someday my ship will come in, but I will probably be at the airport.

Eddie lived with his wife Connie and their four children in a frame house in the mill village in Groveville. He had worked for years at Dixie Textile Corporation, which was one of the major industries in town. He did not waste his money on liquor or cigarettes because he did not participate in either of these activities. Still, Eddie had a hard time making ends meet. He would often lie awake at night and wonder what he could do to better provide for his family. He didn't particularly want to be rich; he just wanted enough to live comfortably.

One day, while he was on a break at work, a co-worker began talking about the state lottery and how he bought lottery tickets each week. Sometimes he would win fifty or a hundred dollars in some of the scratch-off games, but he had never hit a big jackpot. Eddie had never bought a lottery ticket, and he had no intention of buying one. Yet, his friend had planted a seed in Eddie's mind. The fertile dirt in Eddie's brain had already been plowed, and so the seed thought began to germinate in his well-watered brain soil. That is why, a week later, Eddie bought a lottery ticket.

Immediately after purchasing the ticket, Eddie's conscience struck him with guilt. He was a God-fearing worshipper at the First Community Fellowship Church, and in his mind, he knew that what he had done was wrong. His father had instilled in him a strong sense of moral values. When he was growing up, according to his father, there were two things that you did not do if you wanted to escape the damnation of hell. The first of these was the fact that you did not go fishing on Sunday. The second was that you did not gamble. Both of these would incur the wrath of God immediately.

The day after the ticket purchase, Eddie went to see Pastor Laster at the church and told him what he had done. The good pastor was sympathetic to Eddie and reassured him that God still loved him and that he would not go to the lake of fire just because he had bought a lottery ticket. Pastor Laster counseled him about the dangers of gambling and tried to show him why he felt that it was wrong. First of all, he told Eddie about the addictive nature of gambling.

Some folks just didn't know when to stop. Secondly, it promoted a philosophy of luck instead of hard work. Thirdly, it meant that we were trying to provide for ourselves, instead of trusting in God. He encouraged Eddie to not be fooled by worldly doctrines, but to stick to what he felt God would have him do. After the pastor prayed with him, Eddie left feeling somewhat better.

A week later, Eddie asked to speak with the pastor again about gambling. When he came into the pastor's study, Pastor Laster greeted him and once more began to talk to him about the dangers of gambling. However, he was suddenly interrupted by Eddie who said, "Pastor, I remember all that we talked about last week about gambling. I have vowed never to do that again, but, I have just one question for you, sir: What do I do with the two million dollars I won?"

The Letter to the Senator

Sen. Steven Panderhurst, the state senator, liked to keep in touch with his constituents. He always told the people that he had an open door policy as far as meeting their needs and helping to solve their problems. He was always receptive to phone calls and letters from people with ideas on improving the state. As a result of this, he was well thought of, and had been re-elected to four terms of office. One day, as he was reading his mail, he came across a letter from a man named Jimmy Brookshire, who lived in Aardvark County. The letter read like this:

Dear Sen. Panderhurst,

I am writing this letter with the best intentions of offering you some ideas on how we could improve our state. The first thing I would like to mention is my concern over retired teachers' health care. I personally have known several retired teachers who have mentally gone off the deep end. Just last year, I ran across three of my former teachers from when I was in school thirty years ago. It was sad to see what has happened to their minds, for none of them could remember my name. This was upsetting because I was a good student. Some kind of special fund should be established to help these wayward souls out.

Maybe when parents enrolled their children in school each year, they could pay a small fee that would go into this fund to help these retired teachers. You could call it a TIC Tax (Teacher's Insanity Commission). I'm sure this would help take care of those dedicated teachers who have imparted their knowledge to us and our children down though the years. After all, a mind is a terrible thing to waste. And speaking of teachers, shouldn't they be given hazard pay? Their job is more dangerous than being a convenience store clerk on New Year's Eve. I think that they should be more fully compensated for this.

The second area that I think needs some improvement is our dealings with blind people. Now, I think that you will agree with me that the biggest problem for the blind is that they can't see. We need to help these people. I propose that we make stop signs that beep. This way, the blind person can know that he is supposed to stop as he is traveling down the road. Let's face it: stop signs are red and octagonal shaped. But how does the blind man know this? Can a person feel the color red? The only way for a blind person to know there is a stop sign there, is for him to get out of the car and feel the shape of it. This really defeats the purpose, because he has had to stop already anyway.

Another thing we should do for the blind is to have a special blind person's advocate in every store. They could serve as an assistant to help the blind person to make purchases. How does a blind person know what size clothes he or she wears? They can't read the tape measures or the labels in clothes. The special helper could assist with measuring the blind person, so he could be sure to get the right fit in all his clothes. The special assistant could also help with other shopping the blind person needs to do. How does a blind person know the difference between Ben-Gay and Preparation H when it is on the shelf? The assistant could help with this and make the shopping experience more enjoyable.

Thirdly, I think that we need some improvement in our Wildlife Department. I think it should be illegal to catch a fish and then release it. God gave us fish in the rivers, lakes, and oceans so that we could have something to eat. With all the hungry people in the world today, I think it is wrong to catch fish and not eat them. If the fisherman is not going to eat the fish, then at least he should give them away. Jesus did not believe in catch and release. We read in the Bible where He ate fish. In the story where Jesus told the disciples to cast the net on the other side of the boat and they caught a multitude of fish, He did not tell his disciple, "Y'all take a picture of those fish and turn them loose. We will put that picture in the Bible between Psalms and Proverbs."

I have another idea on the subject of wildlife. I think more thought should be given about the placing of deer crossing signs. I have seen several of these signs in Aardvark County. I think the crossings should be moved to a safer place. As it is, too many deer are being killed there.

The last issue I would like to address is one that is my pet peeve. I think there should be a law against people putting up a sign in their yard that reads: 'House for Sale by Owner.' You have to know that the owner is the one selling the thing! You never see a sign that says: 'House for Sale by Renters,' or even, 'House for Sale by Next-Door Neighbors.' I realize that you can't legislate stupidity, but if you could, this would be a good place to start.

As you can see, these are some simple suggestions to improve our state. Believe me, these suggestions come from my heart, because I am a simple-minded man. I will try to rack my brain and come up with some more suggestions, but I cannot guarantee that they will be as good as these.

Sincerely,
Jimmy Brookshire

The Ugly Tie Contest

Pastor Laster was a firm believer in the fact that a church needed fellowship outside of the realm of regular Sunday services. He believed in laughter and really enjoyed joking with people. That is why he tried to have fun events at the church. In addition to homecoming services once a year, the church enjoyed periodical socials and church dinners. In the summer, there was often an ice cream or watermelon eating after the Sunday evening service. Of course, special holidays like Christmas always provided ample opportunities for extra fellowship. An outsider once remarked to Pastor Laster that the church's motto should be: God be with us until we eat again.

One of the church's favorite times of fellowship was the annual ugly tie contest. This was a contest that was thought up by the pastor himself. It took place after the Sunday night service each Father's Day. Most of the time, finger food was served and everyone had a good time. Sometimes, William Smithers would bring another one of his wooden cakes or cement pies and try to fool some unsuspecting lady who tried to slice it.

The idea behind the ugly tie contest was this: It was believed that many fathers received ties for Father's Day just because their kids or wife didn't know what else to buy them. Some of these proved to be less than beautiful. This would be a good time to have a laugh and fellowship together. (By the way, ladies, we men don't usually really need another tie. Wouldn't it be nice if y'all could think up something different as a gift?)

This contest was all done in good fun. This was such a good time for the folks of the church that everyone looked forward to this event. In fact, many of the men visited the thrift stores a few days before the contest, in hopes of securing the perfect ugly tie to bring home the award and bragging rights.

An unusual thing happened at the sixth annual ugly tie contest. Major Ernest Allen (ret. U.S. Army) and his wife Isabel settled in Aardvark County after his retirement. They had traveled through the area before and found it to be a charming place to live. They purchased a house just down the road from the First Community Fellowship Church and had discussed the possibility of worshipping there. Their movers had just arrived and unloaded their belongings the day before. Ernest and Isabel worked hard that weekend putting their things in order. Neither of them went to church that Sunday morning. Ernest decided to check out the church down the road that Sunday evening, but Isabel was too tired to accompany him.

Now, Isabel had given her husband a tie for Father's Day. One of the sad facts of life is that not every gift that looks beautiful to the giver, looks beautiful to the recipient. The tie was an assortment of bright colors intermingled, with no definite starting or stopping point for each one. It just kind of faded together. At the bottom of the tie was a cartoon drawing of a man in a rowboat, catching a tremendously overgrown fish. Ernest was an avid fisherman, so Isabel felt that he would like it. Ernest lied a little and told his wife that the tie was perfect. The only problem was that he didn't say perfect for what.

Ernest figured he would have to wear the tie eventually, so he decided to go ahead and wear it to church that night. When he got to the church, he was warmly welcomed and encouraged to stay for the social afterwards. At this point, both Pastor Laster and the congregation fumbled the ball. Because this was the sixth ugly tie contest, they all just assumed that everyone knew what was about to happen. The fact of the matter was that poor Ernest did not know that he was about to be a contestant in the contest.

After everyone had eaten, the pastor introduced the panel of judges to the congregation. The panel was made up of three outstanding ladies who would decide who would get the blue ribbon. (The award, not the beer.) After a few minutes of walking around, looking, and debating, the ladies unanimously decided that this year's award for the ugliest tie would go to their visitor, Mr. Ernest Allen.

When Ernest got home, he showed his wife the ribbon and told her that he won it at church. Then, as all curious wives would, she asked, "How did you win it?"

Not wanting to hurt her feelings, Ernest replied, "I got it for having the most unique tie."

"That church seems like a fun place to be," said Isabel.

"Yes, Dear," answered Ernest, "I'm sure you'll fit in just fine."

A Thought from Pastor Laster

If absence makes the heart grow fonder, some folks must really be in love with the church.

The Inflation Problem

The Rev. A.T. Laster, though a good pastor, at times, had a tendency to be a little absent-minded. One of his biggest problems was the fact that he often could not remember where he had parked his car. There were a few incidents when he came out of a store and was at a complete loss as to where his car was. The problem was further heightened when big businesses came to Aardvark County. The small, family-run grocery stores gave way to larger supermarkets, which resulted in more cars being parked in the parking lots. Pastor Laster was at a total loss when he went somewhere like Walmart, or when he visited patients in the hospital. Sometimes, he wandered around several minutes, looking for his car.

One time, Pastor Laster was shopping with his wife, Mildred. They had agreed that when each of them was finished shopping that they would meet up at the car. When the pastor came out of the store, he searched diligently for his car. After going up and down several rows, he spied it in the next row. As he neared the vehicle, he noticed, to his horror, that someone had smashed his right rear taillight – obviously a hit-and-run incident. Pastor Laster walked back into the store and called the police. A few minutes later, a police officer arrived on the scene. For some reason, people everywhere are just naturally curious when they see a police officer in a parking lot. Soon, a crowd of people was standing around watching as Pastor Laster explained to the officer how he had been victimized. A few minutes later, Mrs. Laster walked up to the group and said to her husband, "Where in the world have you been? I have been waiting a half-hour for you. Come on! Our car is over here." About that time, the real owner of the car approached the scene and explained to the officer that this was no recent accident; his wife had backed into the mailbox the week before. Pastor Laster sheepishly apologized to the officer and followed his wife to their car.

On another occasion, Pastor Laster once again had a little difficulty locating his car. He had volunteered to pick up a few things at the grocery store for his wife. As he came out of the store, he saw what he thought was his car. He approached the car from the passenger side and tried to put his bags of groceries in the back seat. The back door was locked. Then, he tried to open the front door. He found that it too was locked. Suddenly, he heard the car horn blow. It was then that he saw the elderly lady, with a frightened look on her face, sitting in the driver's seat, ready to drive off.

Incidents like these caused Pastor Laster to do some serious brainstorming about how he could better locate his car in a parking lot. Suddenly, he had one of those "aha" moments of supernatural insight that he felt was nothing short of pure genius. Pastor Laster bought himself a package of red balloons, which he kept in the trunk of the car. Then, when he went into a store, he could tie one of the inflated balloons to his radio antenna. That way, he would just have to look for the car with the red balloon attached.

The pastor's plan worked wonderfully well for a while. Then, after a few weeks, he noticed that a few other folks had stolen his idea and had put balloons on their cars. He didn't realize it at the time, but he had started a new trend. In a little place like Aardvark County, it doesn't take long for a good idea to spread like wildfire. One day about three months after the balloon idea came to Pastor Laster, he once again went shopping with his wife. When he came out of the store, to his amazement, he saw hundreds of red balloons tied on car antennas. Once more, he walked around for a while before he found his car. Once more, he went home to think about his situation. As of yet, he has not found a solution to his problem. Perhaps, some of you good folks can think up something to help him. I'm sure he would appreciate any suggestions.

Mrs. Laster's Ministry

A lot has been said about the Rev. A. T. Laster and his ministry at the First Community Fellowship Church. His ministry was successful for many reasons, but none more important than the fact that he had the support of his wife, Mildred. It was she who made sure that his clothes were clean and pressed, that his meals were cooked, and that he presented himself in a positive way. A husband should never get to the point where he forgets the importance of a dedicated wife. Pastor Laster realized the importance of his wife and often commented that without her, his ministry would be severely lacking.

In addition to being "the minister to the minister," Mrs. Laster somehow found time to be involved in other community services. One of her favorite ministries was her involvement with the mentally ill. She was a volunteer at Herringbone Mental Hospital in Aardvark County. It was here that she helped with the patients – sometimes just visiting and talking with them, and sometimes, assisting them by taking them on walks or helping them with their daily living. She became more than just a volunteer, for she made friends with many of the clients there. She had even been known to keep in touch with clients when they were dismissed from the facility, sometimes helping them find a place to live or a job.

At the hospital, two of the clients were brothers named Gerald and Harold Masterson. Both of these men were bald. One spring day as Mrs. Laster was visiting them, she suggested that they go outside for a walk to get some of the nice fresh air and sunshine.

As they strolled around the grounds, they passed under a big oak tree. Up in the tree, there was a bird, singing beautifully in the spring sunshine. One of the strange things about birds is that, even though they are beautiful creatures, they are not particularly pretty in their bathroom habits. The good thing about birds is that they never have to wait in line to use the bathroom. It just so happened, that as Mrs. Laster and the men passed under the tree, the bird chose that opportunity to take a bathroom break. Unfortunately for Gerald, the bird's relief was his distress, because the bird droppings landed squarely on his bald head.

Mrs. Laster immediately took control of the situation. She told the men, "Do not move! I will run and get some toilet tissue."

After she ran off, Gerald looked at Harold and said, "They put us in here because they say we're crazy. She's the one that's crazy! Doesn't she know that when she gets back here that bird will be long gone?"

After Gerald and Harold continued with their treatments at the hospital for about a year, both of them were declared by their doctors to be "cured" of their illnesses. Mrs. Laster had taken a particular interest in them, and wanted to see the men do well as they were returned to the mainstream of society. Through some connections at church, she had become friends with some of the supervisors at Dixie Textile Corporation. She persuaded the supervisors to try to find jobs for Gerald and Harold. Finally, a suitable job was found for them in the company's warehouse. They were hired as a favor to Mrs. Laster – but only on an experimental basis.

On the first day of work, each of the men reported proudly to the company. They were turned over to another employee who would do their training. Things went really well for a few hours. Then, Gerald and Harold seemed to have a relapse. About twelve o'clock, the boss strolled through the warehouse to check on the situation. At that time, he found Harold hanging from the ceiling, screaming, and saying, "Look at me! I'm a light bulb!"

The boss said, "Harold, you ain't no light bulb! I can't handle this! I will just have to tell Mrs. Laster that this didn't work out. Get down and get your stuff and get out."

So Harold came down from the ceiling, picked up his coat and lunch box, and started toward the door. Gerald picked up his stuff and followed Harold. The boss asked Gerald, "Where are you going? I fired Harold, not you!"

Gerald then replied, "Well, you don't want me to stay and work in the dark, do you?"

Gems of Wisdom
from The Old-Timer

The first sign of severe mental illness is having hair on your thumbs. The second sign is looking to see if you have hair on your thumbs.

Church Visitation

Pastor Laster, of the First Community Fellowship Church, had many pastoral duties. He was the preacher for all the worship services, but he also spent much of his time in church visitation. He would visit the sick, in the hospital or at home, on a regular basis. He also visited with people who were un-churched, so that he could be a witness to them, hoping they would accept Christ as their Savior. While he was confident that he was doing the work of the Lord, there were some times when he felt that he should have just stayed at home.

When Pastor Laster first became the church's pastor, he was fresh out of seminary. He soon found out that the book knowledge he had learned in school, sometimes did not apply to real life situations. The truth of the matter is that there are no textbook cases when it comes to church visitation and witnessing. This is due, in part, to the unpredictability of people's responses. Sometimes, when a pastor thinks he is really making headway in dealing with folks about their relationship with God, they come up with a new response or question. For example, Pastor Laster had been asked, "Where did Cain get his wife?" "How did Noah get all those animals on the ark?" and even, "Just how poor was Job's turkey?"

One day, as he was still honing his people relation skills, he visited a farmer whose name had been given to him by a concerned church member. Pastor Laster walked up to the farmer and introduced himself. Then, he asked the man the question, "Sir, are you a Christian?"

The farmer shook his head and replied, "No, Sir, my name is Jones. Mr. Christian lives about a mile up the road on the left."

Pastor Laster then asked, "You don't understand, Sir; are you ready for the Judgment Day?"

Mr. Jones then said, "I don't know! When is it going to be?"

The preacher responded, "I don't really know; it may be tomorrow or it may be the next day."

Mr. Jones then replied, "Well let us know! I'm sure my wife will want to go both days."

One day, Pastor Laster went to visit a lady who was a church membership prospect. This middle-aged lady had just moved to Aardvark County. She had visited the church a couple of times and heard Pastor Laster preach. The word on the street was that she was looking for a church home. Pastor Laster drove to the lady's house and knocked on the front door. There was no response. He knocked again, but there was still no response. Her car was in the yard, so he felt that perhaps she did not hear his knock. Pastor Laster walked around to the back door and knocked again. Still, there was no response. The preacher pulled one of his business cards out of his pocket, wrote a Bible verse on the back of it, and placed it on the screen door. The verse was Revelation 3:20 which read: Behold I stand at the door and knock: if any man hear my voice, and open the door, I will come in and sup with him, and he with me.

The next Sunday, the woman was once again in the congregation as Pastor Laster preached. After the service, as he greeted everyone at the door, the lady handed the preacher back his business card and walked out the door. On the card, she had scribbled the Bible reference of Genesis 3:10. When Pastor Laster looked up the verse, he found these words: I heard thy voice in the garden, and I was afraid, because I was naked; and I hid myself.

Some of the most enjoyable times in Pastor Laster's ministry were when he had the opportunity to visit the elderly and the shut-ins. There was one dear old lady in the congregation whom everyone called Aunt Het. She had been a faithful church member for years and had at one time been active as a Sunday school teacher. In the last few years, however, she had worshipped at home due to declining health. Pastor Laster loved to visit with Aunt Het. Sometimes, they would sit and talk about the Bible for hours. Often, Pastor Laster found that he had completely lost track of the time and would have to hurriedly excuse himself, so that he could visit others.

One day, as he was visiting with Aunt Het, he noticed a large candy jar full of salted peanuts sitting on her coffee table. As they began to talk, Aunt Het offered him some of the peanuts. Pastor Laster liked peanuts, so he took a few. Peanuts, as you probably know, are habit-forming. No one can eat just one. As the afternoon wore on, Pastor Laster dipped time after time into the candy jar. Soon, he noticed to his surprise, that they had been talking for nearly three hours. He also noticed, shockingly, that he had eaten all the peanuts from the jar.

"Aunt Het," the pastor said sheepishly, "I'm so sorry! Look at what I've done! I've eaten up all of your peanuts."

Aunt Het just smiled and said, "That's all right, Pastor. I was done with them. I sucked all the chocolate off of them yesterday."

A Thought from Pastor Laster
(on church visitation)

You may have the best looking can of worms that money can buy, but that don't mean that the catfish will jump up on the bank to get it.

The Faith Healer

Every now and then, traveling preachers would come through Aardvark County and hold tent revival meetings. Some of these men were actually true preachers of the gospel who shared their message and converted many. There were other preachers, however, that seemed to prey on the emotions and the generosity of the people to be successful financially. Some of these preachers used such tactics as selling blessed prayer cloths (actually, these cloths were just a bunch of handkerchiefs that the preacher had picked up at the 5&10 on the way to town) and other religious relics to support their ministries. The local pastors often had a problem with this group of preachers because they did not seem to focus on the true gospel. Members of the local congregations often attended the tent meetings out of curiosity, and listened to what the traveling preacher had said. Then, they went to their local pastors and told him that "Brother So and So" had said "Such and Such." As a result of this, many believers were left confused. The end result was that the local pastors had to counsel the congregations long after the traveling preacher had collected his offerings, taken down his tent, and left town.

One traveling preacher who came to town was a man who called himself Brother Ben. He searched for a place to set up his tent, and found one in a cut hay field on a farm that belonged to Lewis Richards. Brother Ben felt that the field would be perfect because it was beside the main road that led to Groveville. Lewis had agreed to let Brother Ben hold his meetings there – as long as there would be no snake handling services. The mainstream religious system of Aardvark County didn't cotton much to handling snakes, except for that one church up in the mountains. Brother Ben assured Lewis that he was a gospel preacher and a faith healer, and that he was not, in any way, associated with the snake handlers.

When Brother Ben and his workers arrived in town, he drove a big truck with a sign printed on each side. The signs read: Brother Ben, the Sinner's Friend. In smaller letters was printed: Your Faith Has Made You Whole. The workers set up the tent and unfolded the chairs as the curious townsfolk looked on. For two days after the tent was set up, Brother Ben and his crew passed out flyers, announcing that God was going to do some great healing in the crusade.

Now, I tried not to pass judgment on Brother Ben, but I don't recall where Jesus healed that way. I can't find anywhere in the Bible where Jesus pitched a tent and invited folks to come to a big healing service. In the Bible when Jesus healed people, he met them where they were, or they came and sought him out. Maybe I'm just an old skeptic who is set in his ways, but I reckon that if someone felt that God had given him the gift of healing, he would be wise to do it like Jesus did it.

At the first night of the crusade, the tent was about

half full. Brother Ben was not worried because he knew that it took several days for word to get around about the services. Brother Ben led the music from some old discarded hymnals that had been given to him long ago. He then preached a powerful message about salvation and healing. He extended an invitation for those who needed salvation or physical healing to come forward and be delivered from their infirmities.

Attending the service that night was Lewis Richards, the owner of the "holy ground" on which Brother Ben preached. Lewis got caught up in the preaching service. He also had an ailment, so when the preacher issued the altar call, Lewis went forward to be healed. When he arrived at the altar, he found that he was the fourth person in line. Looking back after the crusade had closed, the local people could not recall ever having seen those first three people in line before, and they thought it was odd that they had not seen them since.

The first man in the prayer line carried a white cane and said he was blind. From his position in line at the altar, Lewis could see everything that happened. Brother Ben asked the man, "Do you believe that God can heal you?"

The man replied, "Yes, Brother, I believe."

Then, Brother Ben placed his hands on the man's head and put his thumbs over the man's eyes. Then he said, "Your faith has made you whole. Be healed!"

Immediately, the man said, "Praise God! I can see." The congregation applauded and shouted praises.

The second person in line was a man who indicated

Brother Ben, the sinner's friend

that he was deaf. Brother Ben laid his hands on the man's head, stuck his fingers in the man's ears, and said, "Be healed!"

The deaf man shouted, "Hallelujah, I can hear." The people were beside themselves, shouting praises for the things they had seen.

The next person in line was a woman. She was bent over and told the preacher that she wanted to be healed so she could stand up straight. Brother Ben placed his hands on her shoulders and gently rubbed the top of her spine with his thumbs. Then, he shouted with a loud voice, "Be healed!" The woman then stood up straight and praised God.

When the woman stood up, Lewis panicked and ran up the aisle to the back of the tent. Brother Ben came to the back of the tent and asked him, "Brother, do you not want to be healed?"

Lewis replied, "Oh yes, Preacher; I believe God can heal me."

"Then what is the problem?" the preacher asked.

"Well preacher," said Lewis; "It's like this. I saw you put thumbs on the blind man's eyes, and he was healed. I saw you put your thumbs in the deaf man's ears, and he was healed. Then, I saw you put your thumbs on the woman's neck, and she was healed. My problem, Sir, is that I have hemorrhoids, and you and your thumbs ain't going to touch me."

Bubba and the Stolen Offering

You probably remember Bubba Brunson and some of the crazy schemes that he came up with. You will recall how Bubba got into trouble with the law because he wanted to name his car repair business "Bubba's Escort Service." After Bubba got over that little escapade, he became a certified mechanic in Aardvark County and built up a profitable business. Now, everyone in Aardvark County knew that Bubba was kind of strange, but everyone loved him anyway. Folks had been known to say, "That Bubba is an odd man, but he really knows how to fix cars."

A person with a brain like Bubba's can't seem to control the impulse to continually think of new schemes. The folks in Aardvark County considered him a dreamer because of all the ideas that he had conjured up. Even after he became a bona-fide mechanic, he thought of ideas to help himself and to benefit (in his opinion) all mankind. One idea that Bubba had was "Dial-a-Date for Dogs," for lonely dogs that needed companionship. The technical name for this service was "The Canine Courtship Club." This idea really didn't go over too good because everyone knows that dogs have unique ways of finding their own dates and companions.

Earlier in his life, Bubba had come up with some

business ideas that had actually provided him with an income. The first one was a lawn-care service. He even came up with a catchy slogan. His slogan was Let Bubba Cut Your Grass, While You Relax And Sit On Your Front Porch.

The second business was a trash collection service. Bubba got an old truck and went around to his customers and hauled their trash to the dump. This business also had a catchy slogan, which involved a guarantee of good service. On the side of Bubba's truck he had painted: Satisfaction Guaranteed or Double Your Garbage Back.

Bubba also had some ideas concerning the food industry. He suggested to a major potato chip manufacturing that they make an extremely big potato chip called "buffalo chips." The company did not like the idea because of its bad connotations, but they wrote Bubba a nice letter explaining that with a potato chip that big, they could not possibly guarantee that it would stay intact during shipping.

Another time, Bubba suggested to a frozen food company that they make a salmon entrée that had been a family favorite from the recipe files of his mother, Ella Brunson. He called the entrée "Salmonella." The frozen food company said, "Thanks, but no thanks."

Another suggestion from Bubba was the time that he recommended to a fast food business that they change the name of their hamburgers to "Golly Whoppers." The company rejected this idea, explaining that they did not want to mess with perfection.

Most of the folks in Aardvark County did not take

Bubba seriously in any of his endeavors. There was a time, however, when Bubba showed that he had a serious and sensitive side – a time when Bubba took something that was intended for someone else and kept it for himself. The thing that Bubba took was part of the church offering. Now, before you kind folks condemn old Bubba for his actions, I think a word of explanation is in order.

As you will recall, Bubba had an ugly sister named Arlene, who married a blind man named Bob Scuttles. Well, Bob and Arlene had a baby girl they named Bobbilene. Because Bubba was never married, he kind of took to Bobbilene, just like she was his own daughter. When she was a child, he sort of filled in as a substitute daddy, often playing games with her. One of her fondest memories was playing in the yard with her Uncle Bubba. It was he who taught her to play baseball. (No disrespect intended, but I have found that – for the most part – blind people like Bob are not very good at baseball.) Bubba and Bobbilene would play for hours, with him trying to teach her to hit and catch the ball. One thing was for certain: Bubba loved Bobbilene and she loved him.

One of the sad facts of life is that children grow up and change interests. The same little girls that played catch and hopscotch as children develop new interests as they go into their teens. Adding to this situation is the fact that often the adults grow busier and are not able to play with the children as much. Anyway, there came a point where Bobbilene and her Uncle Bubba developed different interests and didn't spend as much time together anymore.

When Bobbilene was sixteen years old, she decided to

part company with some of her childhood possessions, like some dolls and games, and give them away. The First Community Fellowship Church took a mission trip each year to the poorer regions of eastern Kentucky and West Virginia, taking loads of food, clothes, and toys. Bobbilene packed up a few boxes of her used toys and asked Bubba to carry them over to the church in his truck. As Bubba was unloading the boxes, something fell from one box that caused a tear to well up in his eyes. It was a child's baseball glove that he had given Bobbilene when she was six years old. Bubba quickly picked up the glove and threw it back in the truck.

Somewhere in Kentucky that year, a child received a brand new baseball glove, but he did not know the story about why he came to have it. If he had received the used glove, he never would have realized the joy that it had brought to two people. As for the pilfered glove, Bubba took it and put it in his desk drawer. Every now and then, he looks at it and is reminded of a simpler time – when little girls still played baseball and grown men still dreamed dreams.

The Baptism Phobia

One of the most special times in the ministry for a pastor is when he gets to have a baptismal service. It is a great joy to see someone come to accept Christ in his life and then go through the waters of baptism. Most pastors and churches have a collection of funny stories about mishaps in the baptismal pool. Pastor Laster was no exception. One of his most memorable ones was when he baptized Jerome Goggins.

Jerome had attended a revival meeting at the First Community Fellowship Church and had accepted Jesus as his savior. Pastor Laster had arranged to have the baptismal service on a Sunday night, about two weeks after Jerome's conversion. Jerome was not the only person to be baptized that night. Five other people had made professions of faith and were being baptized also.

Now, Jerome was a rather large man. He was about six inches taller than the pastor and outweighed him by about fifty pounds. Normally, this would not be a problem. Because every preacher had their technique for baptizing down to a fine art, they were able, most of the time, to accommodate different sized people. On this night, Jerome was the last to be baptized. The pastor did not expect any problems, but sometimes, the unexpected happens.

When Pastor Laster started the baptism, Jerome panicked. Just as the preacher was leaning him back to put him under, Jerome started twisting. He grabbed Pastor Laster, and both of them fell back into the water. Both men struggled to get to their feet, but then fell again. If it were not for the quick efforts of two deacons who helped fish them out, Pastor Laster would have gone down in the church history records as the pastor who really did give his all for his congregation. After the pastor had regained his composure and dismissed the service, he talked with Jerome. Jerome apologized to the pastor. He was very embarrassed about the incident. Pastor Laster assured him that as far as he was concerned, it was a bona-fide baptism, seeing as how Jerome had gone completely under the water. Jerome, however, would have no part with such an idea. He said, "No, Pastor! I feel that I have to be properly baptized for God to accept it. Can we try it again later?"

So it came to be at the next Sunday morning service, Pastor Laster announced that once more they would have a baptismal service that night. He had talked with Jerome extensively during the week and had tried to encourage him not to be afraid of the water.

At the second baptism service, Pastor Laster stood in the pool. Over in the back corner stood a deacon who was ready to offer assistance if he was needed. When Jerome entered the pool, the pastor whispered words of encouragement to him. As he began the baptism, once again, Jerome panicked. He twisted and grabbed for the pastor. The preacher did a little side step move and dropped Jerome. This time, the pastor did not fall, but Jerome managed to rip his baptismal robe right down the front.

After the service Pastor Laster asked Jerome, "Jerome, what in the world is the matter with you? How could a man as big as you be afraid of the water?"

Jerome replied, "I don't know, Pastor. It seems that going into that little pool frightens the daylights out of me."

Suddenly a light bulb went off in the pastor's ministerial brain. He said, "Jerome, do you ever go swimming?"

Jerome answered, "Yes, sir; I go swimming in the lake and river all the time."

Then, the pastor said, "Then that's it! You're not afraid of water. You're afraid of small places. You have claustrophobia."

At the end of the next Sunday morning service, Pastor Laster announced, "Folks, we have tried to baptize Jerome Goggins twice already. We think we have found an answer to the problem. We are going to baptize Jerome in the creek out back. Those of you who want to see this, come with us out back after we dismiss."

The whole congregation followed the pastor to the creek where the Rev. Bass, the church's first pastor, had baptized people many years before. Pastor Laster waded out into the creek, and Jerome followed him. Then and there, Jerome Goggins was baptized officially and properly into the fellowship of the church.

Even this baptism had a surprise ending. Jerome had always been an avid fisherman. His fishing technique was unusual, though. He liked to go gravelling for fish. This meant that he waded into the water and bare-handedly grabbed the fish. He often found large catfish or bass near submerged brush piles or up near the bank hanging out under tree roots. As he and the preacher were coming up out of the water, he felt the movement of a large fish near his foot. He reached down and pulled up what appeared to be about a four-pound catfish. He was all smiles as he held the fish up. His smile quickly faded, though, when he saw the congregation looking at him. Jerome bent down to the water and let the fish go. Turning to the preacher he said, "I'm sorry, Pastor; I forgot that I don't fish on Sunday anymore."

For years after that, when Pastor Laster would talk to fellow pastors and fishers of men, he would tell about the big one that he caught and the big one that got away.

Benjy's New Job

Benjamin Harrison Jackson III was born September 3, 1945, on Labor Day. He was immediately called Benjy to distinguish him from his grandfather Benjamin Harrison Jackson, Sr., who was called Ben, and from his father Benjamin Harrison Jackson, Jr., who was called B.H. He came from a family of blue-collar working people. His grandfather had been a carpenter in the early years of the twentieth century. He had been under contract with Dixie Textile Corporation to build outhouses for the houses that the mill owned. When indoor plumbing became the modern way to go, the mill houses were remodeled to accommodate inside bathrooms. Because of this, Ben took on other carpentry jobs because the outhouse business had gone in the hole.

B.H. continued in his father's footsteps, and he too, became a carpenter. He helped build houses in the suburbs after World War II. Americans were feeling good about themselves because they had overcome the Great Depression and had defeated the Germans and Japanese in the war. There was a general feeling of prosperity, and folks began to want nicer houses. Thus, there was plenty of work for B.H. all of his adult life.

It was ironic that Benjy was born on Labor Day because

labor was not something that he was interested in. The family's work ethic genes did not filter down to him. It was known around Aardvark County that Benjy was not exactly the sharpest tool in the shed, mentally. He had potential, but he never seemed to apply himself. In his mind, the reason he had taken fourteen years to get his high school diploma was because all of his teachers were against him. He figured it was his lot in life to be surrounded by "sorry teachers" who really didn't understand him.

Unlike his father and grandfather, Benjy did not like carpentry. He just could not get the hang of cutting boards straight or figuring out what angle to cut rafters for the proper slope. Even in his high school shop class, the small projects that he made, such as birdhouses and toolboxes, looked like they had been made by a Vacation Bible School craft class dropout. So it was then, that Benjy had a succession of jobs through his early years. He would begin a job with good intentions, but soon realize that he would rather be fishing or playing baseball with his friends. Bosses usually have a rule that employees need to show up for work to accomplish anything; so many times, Benjy was told that his services were no longer needed.

About the time that Benjy celebrated his thirtieth birthday, he had a hankering once again that he should seek employment. After all, he could retire in thirty-five years, but he didn't have anything to retire from. Coincidently, about this time, Dixie Textile Corporation announced that they would soon have an opening as a supervisor, due to a retirement. Textile operations, by this time, had become sophisticated, so the company wanted someone who had some technical knowledge, was fairly intelligent, and had some supervisory experience. One of the good things about being a lazy person is that they can usually think of creative ways to make themselves look good. Such was the case with Benjy Jackson. He applied for the job and listed his work experience as having been a pilot, a pharmacist, and as having supervisory experience. Amazingly, he was granted an interview with the personnel director.

The personnel director, Mr. James Bledsoe, was fairly new to Aardvark County, so he wasn't very familiar with a lot of the local residents. In particular, he had never met Benjy Jackson. At the interview, Mr. Bledsoe began to talk to Benjy about the job responsibilities. Benjy assured him that he was well qualified to handle the position. When Mr. Bledsoe began to talk about past job experience, however, the interview began to go downhill. When Benjy was asked about the pilot's job, he told Mr. Bledsoe about the time he had worked at Ed Jenkins horse farm. His job was to clean out the horse stalls. He would rake the manure, shovel it, and "pile it." Therefore, he called himself a "pilot."

By this time, Mr. Bledsoe realized that he was talking to someone whose elevator did not go to the top floor where the brains were supposed to be stored. He should have stopped the interview then, but he was curious about what Benjy would say next. He then asked about the pharmacist job. Benjy told him about the time he had gone to work on the Colin Brown farm. His job there had been to milk the cows, pitch the hay, and generally assist the farmer with his chores. So he called himself a "farm-assist" person.

Mr. Bledsoe then asked Benjy, "In light of your other two jobs, how could you have possibly have had supervisory experience?"

"Well," said Benjy, "it happened when I was working at the Celestial Valley Funeral Home and Wedding Chapel. I had a job over hundreds of people. They let me cut the grass in the cemetery."

The director then told him, "Mr. Jackson, I feel that a man of your talents would be dissatisfied with a job such as this. However, we do have an opening that will suit you, if you are interested." So it came to pass that Benjy Jackson went to work the next day in the weaving department of Dixie Textile as a floor sweeper. He kept thinking about how Mr. Bledsoe had called him "Mr. Jackson." Nobody had ever called him that before. It gave him a new sense of direction concerning work. Benjy did not try to move up the ladder of success at the mill. This was the job his friend, Mr. Bledsoe, had given him, so he worked it faithfully for twenty-five years, until the plant closed due to economic conditions.

Woes of the Preachers

One of the most appreciated aspects of Pastor Laster's ministry among his congregation was his visitation of the sick. He was often seen at the Aardvark County Hospital visiting his people when they were sick or having surgery. He was there with the family, sitting with them during their loved ones' surgeries, praying with them, and offering his support. Because of this ministry, he knew most of the doctors, nurses, and employees of the hospital. He was also familiar with the cafeteria staff, whom he visited on a regular basis, especially when they were cooking up some fried chicken or banana pudding.

Although he had been a regular visitor at the hospital for years in a moral support capacity, Pastor Laster had never been a patient. That is, until one night when he was stricken with sharp pains in his right side. The emergency room doctor diagnosed him as having appendicitis and ordered an emergency operation. The operation went well, but the pastor was confined to the hospital for a few days.

Back in those days, the hospitals were set up as semi-private facilities. This meant that there were two people in each room. Pastor Laster's roommate was a man named Charlie Black who had surgery to have a hernia repaired. The two men struck up a friendship and spent many hours talking.

One of the things that Pastor Laster detested about his hospital stay was the fact that he had to wear those short hospital gowns. They never seemed to be long enough to cover the subject. On the second day of his recovery, a new nurse came into the pastor's room. He was still a little groggy from his pain-killing medicine and probably wasn't thinking properly. All he knew was that he felt self-conscious about lying there in that gown. When the nurse came into his room, he reached down and pulled his sheet up securely under his chin.

The nurse looked at Pastor Laster and then asked him, "Mr. Laster, do you feel okay today?" (They always call you "Mister" when you're in the hospital.)

"Well," replied the pastor, "That remains to be seen."

The preacher then heard the nurse say, "I really don't think there is anything left to be seen."

After the nurse left, Charlie asked the preacher, "Man, are you crazy?"

The pastor responded, "Why do you ask?"

Charlie then said, "Just look what you've done!"

Pastor Laster looked and found that instead of pulling up the sheet, he had got hold of his gown tail and pulled it up to his chin. The preacher turned red and each time that the nurse came in after that, he was too embarrassed to even speak to her. She never did find out why Mr. Laster went public with his privates, but she just chalked it up as another instance of why people said that hospital was an interesting place to work.

While Pastor Laster was recovering from his surgery,

The First Community Fellowship Church deacons secured the services of another preacher to fill the pulpit for a couple of Sundays. They arranged for the Rev. Ben Goode to come and preach for them. The Rev. Goode was from Bovine County, just across the line from Aardvark County. He had been retired as a pastor for many years, but was available for supply work as opportunities arose.

On his first Sunday at the church, he had driven the twenty-five miles from his home and arrived at the church with a little bit of time to spare. Just before he got out of his car, he checked his rear-view mirror to see if his hair needed combing or if anything else about his appearance needed his attention. Suddenly, a shock of horror went through his soul, for he realized that he had left his dentures at home. There was nothing he could do now, but he realized that he might not be able to preach properly. He imagined that he would forever be known as that gum-bumper preacher.

As the Rev. Goode walked to the front door of the church, he was greeted by Stanley Anderson, the chairman of the deacons. Stanley's family had been charter members of the church. He, himself, had attended there most of his life, except when he served in the Army during WWII. After his military service, he had gone back to school, gotten married, and raised a family. For many years he had been a successful businessman. Now, he was approaching retirement age.

As Stanley shook hands with the preacher, the Rev. Goode told him, "I don't think I'll be able to preach very well today. You see, I seem to have left my dentures at home."

Stanley then replied, "Well, maybe I can be of assistance." Then he reached in his coat pocket and pulled out a baggie that contained a complete set of dentures. "Here, try these," he said as he handed the bag to the preacher.

The Rev. Goode tried the dentures, but they were too tight. He told Stanley, "I appreciate it, Brother, but these teeth are too tight. I'll sound like I'm from up north if I wear these things."

Stanley then reached in his pocket and produced another set of dentures and gave them to the preacher. "Here, try these then," said Stanley.

The Rev. Goode tried those dentures, but they were too loose. "No," said the preacher, "these won't work either. They're so loose; I'll sound like a drunk when I try to talk."

Once more, Stanley reached into his pocket and produced another set of dentures. When the preacher tried them, they fit just right. He told Stanley, "Brother, I think with these teeth, I might just be able to preach after all."

And so, that day, the Rev. Goode preached confidently and really brought a good message. After the service, everyone shook his hand and told him how much they appreciated him being there. Finally, after everyone else had gone, he approached Stanley and said, "I appreciate you loaning me these dentures. I don't know how I would have made it without them. I sure was lucky that God directed me to meet a dentist like you."

A puzzled look came over Stanley's face, and he replied, "Preacher, you've got it all wrong! I thought you knew. I'm not a dentist; I'm an undertaker."

Gems of Wisdom
from The Old-Timer

Beware when your doctor says that you are a tough old cookie. Everyone knows that when a cookie gets old, it starts to crumble.

The Last Request

Even though Aardvark County had many fine Christian people living there, liquor drinking was often a problem. Years ago, the moonshine business had prospered, but was now almost non-existent. Still, there were a fair share of bars in the county, and most of them seemed to do good business. Preachers preached against the evils of drinking; parents cautioned their children against it; men lost their jobs and families because of it, but still, the liquor business continued.

There were three attitudes toward liquor drinking in Aardvark County. The first one was that the consumption of alcoholic beverages in any form was wrong. This vein of thinking had a wide range of views in itself. There were those among the teetotalers that had an attitude of tolerance – not drinking themselves, but not dictating what other folks did. On the other end of the spectrum, there were those who refused even to go into a restaurant that served liquor or beer and felt that other Christians should feel the same way.

One of members of this latter group was Calvin Belcher, the young ministerial student from Pastor Laster's church. Calvin's mother had bought a new tablecloth from the 5&10. At the time, she did not know that Calvin would go bonkers when he saw it, but that is exactly what he did. Mrs. Belcher did not have many nice things, and so she thought the pretty tablecloth would add a touch of elegance to her simple house. The design was a French scene, with a bottle of wine, a chunk of cheese, and a loaf of bread on a table. Calvin, when he saw it, informed her that no decent Christian family would have such thing as this on their table. He further told her that he thought it was the devil's tablecloth. He raised such a fuss, his mother took the tablecloth back and exchanged it for one with daisies on it. That was fine with Calvin, for daisies were cool.

The second attitude of drinking was that a little alcohol was okay. This was the group of people who felt that it was okay to drink occasionally. They were what are called the social drinkers. Many of these people were church-goers, but they felt that occasionally a "little toddy for the body" was fine. This group also included the working folks, who sometimes stopped at a bar after work to toss down a few. Into this group of people fell a man named Norman Adams.

Norman was in the construction business, having moved to Aardvark County from Ohio. On his first day there, he discovered Joe's Place, a neighborhood bar and grill. After work one day, Norman went to Joe's and ordered three mugs of beer. Joe, the bartender, thought that this was mighty odd, as most people would order just one beer, drink it, and then get another. Norman continued this practice for about a week. Finally, Joe's curiosity got the best of him and so he asked Norman, "Why do you buy three beers at a time, instead of just one"?

Norman replied, "Well, you see, I had these two friends

back in Ohio, and every day we would go out after work and drink a beer. I miss them terribly, so I come in here each day and set up their beers and drink them in their honor. It helps me cope with my homesickness."

This went on several weeks, but one day, Norman changed his routine and just ordered two beers. Naturally, Joe was concerned because Norman had become his friend. When Norman got ready to leave, Joe asked him, "Hey, Pal, I noticed that you just ordered two beers today. Did something happen to one of your friends?"

Joe replied, "Oh, no, they're both fine back there in Ohio."

Then Joe asked, "But why did you just drink two beers instead of three?"

Norman responded, "I only needed two today. You see, I gave up drinking."

The third attitude about drinking in Aardvark County was that liquor drinking was a profession. These were the professional drinkers who were called such names as alcoholics, winos, drunks, sots, and lushes. Many of these people had lost their families due to their drinking, yet they continued their downward spirals. Such was the case of Jerry and Jimmy Tucker. They were brothers and two of the most infamous winos in Aardvark County. One day Jerry got sick and had to go to the doctor. After running some tests, the doctor had some bad news. "Jerry," he said, "I'm afraid I have to tell you that you have cirrhosis of the liver."

Jerry asked, "Okay, Doc, what does that mean in simple English?"

"Well," replied the doctor, "it means that you have drunk so much that you have burned out your guts. At the most, I would say that you six weeks to live."

That night, as he lay in bed, Jerry thought about what the doctor had said. The next morning, he phoned his brother and told him the news. Then he said, "Jimmy, we've had some good times together. We've drunk a lot of liquor and wine, and now it has ruined my health and soon will cost me my life. I have a request for you. When I die, every week I want you to buy a bottle of the best wine you can find and pour it on my grave to honor me."

There was silence on the other end of the line, and then Jimmy replied, "Okay, Brother, I'll do it, but do you mind if I run it through my kidneys first?"

*"When I die, every week I want you to buy a bottle of wine
and pour it on my grave."*

Technology Comes to
Aardvark County

When a person thinks about Aardvark County, he may get the impression that the residents are a bunch of hill-billy-type people who have no modern conveniences. That is not true! Aardvark County people have a rich cultural heritage of being descended from a simple working-class people, but they also had the privilege of using the technology that had developed through the years. A newspaper reporter who was doing a series on rural American communities summed it up well when he said, "The folks of Aardvark County are a simple people who have been dragged, kicking and screaming, into a modern society, yet still live about a half step behind the rest of the world."

If you took a tour of New York City, you would likely visit the Statue of Liberty, the Empire State Building, or maybe see a Broadway play. If you toured Washington, DC, you would probably visit the Washington Monument, the White House, the Capitol, and all the other famous buildings and monuments. If you were a tourist in Aardvark County, you would probably be encouraged to visit the county museum, where an actual moonshine still that was confiscated in 1921 is on display. You could also visit the Aardvark County Speedway, where each Saturday night, adventurous souls drove their resurrected wrecks around the half-mile dirt track. Perhaps you could visit the county fair, where kids ate too much cotton candy and rode rides until they threw up. By far, the biggest attraction in Aardvark County would be a site that the residents were most proud of. That would be the Walmart store.

When Walmart Corporation announced that they were going to build a store in Aardvark County, everyone was really excited. Nothing like this had ever happened before. It took a year for the store to be completed, but finally, the day came when it opened its doors for business. It seemed like everyone in the county showed up on opening day. Everyone walked the aisles to see what the store had to offer. Everywhere you looked, you saw people standing with their mouths open, amazed at the new store. This was utter fascination. Where else could you buy Oreo cookies and a six-pack of BVDs under the same roof? Or where else could you buy flowers for your dear and guns to kill another kind of deer, all in the same building? Yes, thanks to Walmart, the people of Aardvark County had arrived.

On the first day of store operation, Luanne Chester and her son Jonathan, who was age ten at the time, came to check out the situation. Jonathan was intrigued by all the fine things for sale. After about an hour of walking up and down the aisles, he had to use the restroom. He was gone so long that his mother started to worry about him. When he finally returned about thirty minutes later, she asked him, "Why were you gone so long?"

"Well," he replied, "I was waiting on the employees to

come in."

"What do you mean?" his mother asked.

Jonathan then responded, "The sign on the wall plainly said 'Employees must wash hands.' I kept waiting, but no employees came in. I finally washed my own hands and came on out."

Like in any town in America, technology became progressively more advanced for the people of Aardvark County. The big television sets of the fifties gave way to smaller ones. Cars became more advanced. Folks saw their way through the rise and decline of musical entertainment appliances. They saw the demise of vinyl albums and eight-track tapes. They lived through the cassette era and saw it slowly fall to the advent of CDs. People began to live in a fast-paced microwave society. One of the biggest changes in technology involved personal communications. The telephone system evolved from the crank phones on the wall, to black rotary phones, to push button phones in modern colors, to the invention of cellular phones. Now, because everyone carried a phone with them, there was no need to wait for a call at home. The cell phone, alone, probably did more than any other instrument to cause America to become a mobile society.

Joe Conyers was a good example of how cell phones play an important part in the business communication world. Joe was in the construction business and was the CEO of Conyers Builders. He used his cell phone daily, as much as his workers used building tools. Joe often held open house on weekends for the houses he had built, so the cell phone helped him tremendously to communicate with his customers.

Mack and Anna Sparks moved to Aardvark County from Enoree, South Carolina, and were looking to buy a house. One Sunday afternoon, Mack and Anna toured a house that had been built by Conyers Builders. This was the first day that this house was available for showing because it had only been finished the day before. Unfortunately, in their haste to get the house ready, a worker had dropped and broken the bathroom commode. This was unknown to Joe, as he was out of town that Saturday on business.

Mack and Anna really liked the house, but they noticed that the commode was missing. Anna was a dainty, refined lady, who would have been embarrassed to talk about such a personal item as a commode. She decided to send Joe a text message. The message read: Mr. Conyers, where is the BC?

When Joe got Anna's message he was puzzled. He considered himself to be text message savvy, but he had no idea that BC stood for bathroom commode. He racked his brain, trying to figure out in text lingo exactly what BC stood for. Suddenly, an idea hit him like a lightning bolt, and he realized that BC probably stood for Baptist church. He promptly texted Anna with this message: Mrs. Sparks, you do not have to worry about a BC. You will find that there is a very nice one about a mile down the road from the house. You can't miss it. It is a large building made of red brick sitting there on the left side of the road. There are plenty of good parking spaces available. There is a handicapped entrance for those who have trouble getting in by themselves. The people who go there are very friendly and will probably greet you at the door with a handshake. I'm looking forward to sitting there with your family next Sunday.

Gems of Wisdom
from The Old-Timer

Why is it so hard to operate those new-fangled inventions that are supposed to make our lives easier?

Mr. John

When Pastor Laster first came to The First Community Fellowship Church, he became acquainted with Mr. John Loutin. This was the same man who always brought his dog with him to church. After that first embarrassing incident, on Pastor Laster's first day as pastor of the church, he and Mr. Loutin had become friends. The preacher had visited with him often, and like everyone else in the community, called him "Mr. John."

Now, Mr. John was a God-fearing man who lived life to the fullest. He had been a member of the First Community Fellowship Church for more than forty years and was highly respected and revered. Although he did not try to preach to folks, everyone knew that he was on the Lord's side. You did not have to talk to him very long before you realized that this was one man who really had victory. It seemed, at times, that his one pleasure in life was to make people smile and laugh. He had an unusual sense of humor and was always able to joke with people – even in adverse circumstances.

Mr. John had no family. He had at one time been married, but the marriage ended in an abrupt divorce. He often told people that he had a dearly departed wife. When they began to offer their condolences, he would just smile and say, "Oh, she didn't die, she just departed one day." He considered the folks at the church his family, so they all looked after each other. They would check on him from time to time, and he would provide them with a steady stream of kind words, vegetables from his garden, and candy for the children. His one companion in life, since his retirement, was his old hound dog, Buster. It was Buster who accompanied him to church on Sundays. (Actually, Buster was more faithful than some of the regular members.) They lived their lives like this for fifteen years, with Buster serving his master, and Mr. John serving his Master. But men grow older and so do dogs, so it came to pass that Buster developed a severe incurable parasitic condition and had to be sent to his own "happy hunting ground."

Because Mr. John had no living relatives, he entrusted Pastor Laster with his last wishes concerning his funeral arrangements. With the help of the director from the Celestial Valley Funeral Home and Wedding Chapel, he had made his arrangements a full five years before his demise. His plans were on file at the funeral home, as well as in the pastor's desk. Mr. John was determined that when it came time for him to die, there was going to be a sense of victory in his funeral service. He did not want it to be a sad time with a lot of crying, but rather, a time of celebration over the fact that he had left the sorrows of this life and moved to his heavenly home. He firmly believed that you could have victory in death, as well as in life, so he set about trying to make sure that his memorial service reflected his feelings.

Mr. John had two hobbies in his later years. The first one was gardening, which supplied his friends and him with fresh vegetables. The second hobby was woodworking. He had a talent for creating things from wood that really looked better than store-bought items. One day, Mr. John saw an ad in a catalog that told how to get plans to make your own casket. He really thought that it would be a neat thing to do, so he ordered the plans, along with the necessary hardware and liners for the project. When it was completed, he was allowed to store the casket at the funeral home until the appointed time.

A few years later, he developed cancer and suffered with it for almost a year. When he felt that the end was near, he arranged for his headstone to be carved. The inscription read:

Here lie the remains of John Loutin. He went to Heaven shoutin'

His race on earth has been run; He moved up to Heaven in 1991.

On a sunny spring day, at the time of year when students were receiving their diplomas, Mr. John graduated from this life to his eternal home. His funeral service is still talked about in Aardvark County to this day, because folks had never seen anything like it before. In his coffin, there was a small wooden sign that Mr. John had carved with a message on it. The sign read: Here lies John, stiff as a board, but he's not here; he's with the Lord. On the lid of the casket, he had carved a phrase that he had borrowed from a Martin Luther King, Jr. speech and amended slightly. The carving read: Free at last, free at last, Thank God Almighty, I'm free at last.

Pastor Laster spoke to the packed church about the life that Mr. John had lived and how he knew where his final destination was. He also encouraged others to believe in the same God that Mr. John knew. He then produced a letter that Mr. John, himself, had written to be read at the service. Although Mr. John didn't want people to cry, tears were flowing freely as the pastor read the letter. It said:

Dear friends,

I want to thank each of you who are gathered here today for your loving kindness and for the friendship we have experienced through the years. If you are here today and don't really know me well, I want to assure that because of my faith in my God, at this moment, I am resting and not roasting; I am praising and not parching; I am singing and not sizzling; I am being blessed and not barbequed. I would like to share a poem with you that I ran across one day. It is called "Don't Be Sad "and it goes like this:

Don't be sad when bad things come your way;
Happiness means that we know that tomorrow is a brand new day.
Don't be sad about choices that you've made;
When life deals you a bunch of lemons,
Then you can make lemonade.
Don't be sad when folks are mean and make life hard to live.
When their words cut to the bone, be the better person

and say, "I forgive."
Don't be sad when things don't go as planned.
There's a new adventure around every curve in the road,
So say a prayer and do the best that you can.
Don't be sad when a loved one dies,
For through the tears we must realize,
That this is not the final good-bye.
Don't be sad when it comes your time to go.
Put a smile on your face so others will know,
That in running your race you've done your best,
And that by God's grace you have been blessed.

I don't want to wish any of you any bad luck, but I'm looking forward to seeing you again real soon. By the way, did you hear about the conversation the seven-year-old boy had with his mother? He asked her, "Mom, is it true that from dust we are made, and from dust we will return?" She replied, "That is very true, Son. Why do you ask?" The boy responded, "I just looked under my bed, and there is somebody under there, but I don't know if he's coming or going."

Y'all keep smiling! See you later.
John

When Pastor Laster finished the service, the funeral director wheeled the casket up the aisle. During this time, according to Mr. John's request, the pianist played "Pomp and Circumstance," the graduation music, once more signifying that he had victory and believed that he had graduated to his heavenly home. When the casket was placed in the hearse, Mr. John had arranged to bring one more smile to the faces of his friends. For there on his coffin, for the entire world to see, was a bumper sticker that said *HONK IF YOU LOVE JESUS*. There was only one mistake during the whole service. Happy Mary's Florist had a new employee. There was a mix-up in the flower arrangements. A local grocery that moved to a bigger building received a wreath that said Rest in Peace, while Mr. John received a potted plant that said Good Luck in Your New Location. Mr. John would have loved that!

Special Message from Pastor Laster

If you want to know what folks will be saying about you when you're dead, find out what they are saying about you now. The two should be the same.

Concluding Remarks
from The Old-Timer

I want to thank you kind folks for listening to my stories today. I think that y'all are a fine bunch of people, no matter what your neighbors say about you. I guess that's about all I can remember about these Aardvark County people for now. Maybe, if you come back to see me one day, then I can rack my brain and remember some other stuff about the good people here. There's always something going on here.

Well, it's Saturday afternoon, and I need to hurry over to Shorty's Barbershop and see who's over there telling lies today. I sure hope Pastor Laster doesn't show up. When he comes in for a haircut, we all call it the Pastor Laster Disaster. When we see him coming, we all just automatically go into the Bible story-telling mode. The problem is that some of us get the facts a little mixed up, and he has to tell us the story properly. I bet he wonders why we're always sitting around the barbershop telling Bible stories. I bet he also wonders why we always let him go first.

Perhaps some of you nice people would like to move here. There are just two things that we need more of. One of them is water, for we are in a drought. The second thing is more nice folks to come here. Of course, Pastor Laster keeps reminding us that that's what hell needs too.

Anyway, it's been fun! If you can't come back soon, then please write me. Just make sure you write slowly, because I have always been a slow reader.

Your friend,
The Old-Timer

About the Author

Grover Lawrence lives with his lovely wife, Luanne, and wonderful dog, Daisy, in Woodruff, SC. He has been attempting to make people laugh for years. Only recently has he endeavored to put his humor in print. He also has begun to share stories from his book in live appearances. He has performed in front of many groups including church and retirement facilities. He has also performed in country music venues where he has been publicly compared to Jerry Clower. He has a reputation for telling good, wholesome, family-oriented stories. He is a bonafide member, in good standing, of West End Baptist Church in Woodruff, SC. Grover is available for public appearances at festivals, church groups, and anywhere a group of people need a laugh. He can be reached by telephone at 864-476-2953, by e-mail at aardvarkcounty@gmail.com, or through the following mailing address: P.O. Box 1231, Woodruff, SC, 29388.

About the Illustrator

Samuel Ricketts is a freelance artist who lives in Pelzer, SC. His artwork has received rave reviews in various competitions. He is the designer of Sam's Cards, which is his own hand-drawn greeting card line.

www.ingramcontent.com/pod-product-compliance
Lightning Source LLC
Chambersburg PA
CBHW070454260626
47161CB00004B/1303